Replacing Ann

Beth Durham

Beth Durham

Deut 32:7

Chapter 1

Winnie tripped through the front door with tears in her eyes. Mother's concern was immediate and she wrapped an arm around her second oldest daughter as she asked, "Whatever has happened in the chicken coop to bring on these tears?"

With a sniff, Winnie held up the hem of her dress showing a long tear.

"Why are you a'wailin' over this old rag?"

Winnie looked at her mother, wondering that she had to ask. "It's the only one I have."

Mother smiled in her understanding way. "I can have that stitched 'fore you can even say 'chicken coop'." In moments Mother had repaired the faded cotton garment. The dress wasn't new when her oldest sister wore it and it had been handed down twice since. Now it was soft as down and just as shapeless.

"Your Father should be home any day now. Maybe he'll bring us some dress goods and I'll make new dresses for all three of my girls. The boys sure could use some new things as well."

Winnie listened, while scrubbing the plain kitchen as she was expected to do every morning. Mother had told them many times that they could not control their fortune but they could certainly control the dirt. She looked around the sparsely furnished, rented house. Her mother was the only woman in the community still cooking over a big, open fireplace. Every home Winnie ever chanced to visit boasted a cast iron stove. But Father said they could never tote a heavy thing like that when they moved – and they moved often. In fact, almost every time Father was home for more than a few days, he packed the family to a new place. He never tried to explain why and the children had long since learned to avoid the tongue-lashing, or belt-lashing, that questions brought on.

But Mother would answer questions and so Winnie challenged her optimistic assumption. "What makes you think he'll be here soon?"

"Well dear, it's been near three months this time. That's about as long as he's ever away."

Winnie winced at her mother's delicate reference to Father's absence. He was surely off with some woman, or maybe he'd earned a few dollars and followed some gambling man to try to triple the money; at least those were the theories she heard her older brothers put forth. Father always seemed to have a little money jingling in his pockets despite the bare cupboards from which Mother was expected to produce meals for his eight children. Father came and went faster than the seasons. He was wildly successful at everything he turned his hand to and yet somehow the family remained in poverty. They owned large and prosperous farms but could no sooner get settled than he sold the land to go off to points they never knew of. He opened stores that thrived even when the surrounding communities seemed to have little money to spend. But his own children remained barefoot and ragged.

However, the Lewises were doing okay this time. Summer was winding to a close and the boys had been getting good work splitting fence rails and picking up potatoes at the big potato farm. The youngest of the three was really too young to be in the woods with them and he surely couldn't swing an axe. But Lou and Jimmy assured their sisters that Harry was most helpful in dragging and stacking the finished rails. They were paid a penny for each rail they could finish and most days they could bring home a dollar which kept the family in cornmeal and lard. They had even been able to buy the four chickens that were laying so well. Along with the wild vegetables and berries Mother had taught them all to harvest, it had not been a hungry summer. Of course there was nothing laid by for the cold winter months that were quickly coming upon them. Still, Mother had faith that God would see them through. She kept reminding them that "we haven't starved yet".

"Mother, why do you keep having faith in him? We could leave you know. Women are doing that these days. I'll bet you could get work in one of the big houses in town – nobody keeps a better house than you. Just imagine what you could do if you actually had good furniture and floors without cracks and such."

Again, there was that understanding smile. "Winnie child, I don't have faith in your father, I have faith in my heavenly father. None of us can change your father but we know for sure that God is in control of all these things and He will see us through."

Winnie truly didn't want to argue yet she found herself continuing the questions. "Mother, we have nothing. You scrub and clean this ole' shack till every inch is spotless and you wash and patch our clothes until they are nothing but faded rags. Where is God in all of this?"

Mother reared back as though she might strike her impertinent daughter. "Winifred Lewis, I ought to wash your mouth with lye soap! Where is God you ask, well who do you think keeps us able to work and gives your brothers' a chance to bring home some money? Where do you think the wild lettuce, creases and blackberries come from? Is this not God caring for us every day?"

"But why does God allow Father to sell off good land or close up worthwhile businesses only to go off and squander all of the money? Aren't you ashamed of him?"

"Winnie, I will hear no more slander against your father. You let the good Lord deal with him and we'll all be the better for it. As for being ashamed, there is no shame in being poor. You just always remember, *patches are honorable as long as they're clean.*"

Chapter 2

Bill Lewis wiped the grime from his whiskers as he looked at the steep slope of the road ahead. "Wish I had that horse 'bout now," he said to the vacant lane. Five days ago he rode into Knoxville astride a fine sorrel mare. He sat in one of the most comfortable saddles he'd ever known. The card game had first cost the horse, then hoping to recover his loss and unable to use the saddle alone, he bet and quickly lost the saddle too.

After a hard night on a corner of the train depot's platform, he managed to hop on a westbound train. The train ride hadn't lasted past Harriman where the railroad bull pulled him off and firmly deposited him in the cinders. Nearly broke, it seemed like time to go home. That was two days ago and climbing the mountain from Harriman had been much more effort than Bill planned.

He could scarcely recall how long he'd been away from his mountain home and the family he left there. Of course, he didn't try too hard to count the weeks because he'd seldom thought of the family since he left. His mind was too involved in the people that filled his days and the business ventures he considered and of course the cards he played.

Now it's time to go see what kind of trouble Nadine's let that bunch get into. He allowed his mind to turn to the family, to the wife that was always there waiting and even welcoming him home. Nadine certainly was steady. She was faithful to his children, even the two that weren't her own.

Thinking of Naomi and Jimmy, his oldest children, always turned his thoughts to Ann. Dear, precious Ann, he thought as a tear threatened to escape the corner of his eye.

Our Naomi is on her own now, you know. Bill's thoughts often felt like conversations with his first wife. *I think she's made a fine marriage – she certainly married into a respected family. They've had all kinds of property for years. Jimmy may have left home by now. It's time I guess, he's eighteen years old. I think that Nadine has held on too tightly to him even if he wasn't her own. Don't know why she wants him working and bringing home money or game to her table.*

Of course he heard no answer from the long-dead spouse. The absence of his beloved Ann was one time span that his mind readily recalled. Seventeen years ago she had asked him to go for the granny-woman, announcing it was time for their baby to come into the world. By the time Bill returned to their neat little house, Ann lay on the floor pale and bloodied. He would never understand how that beautiful creature could fade away so quickly. He had not tarried in bringing help; the trip had not been long. The midwife cut into his wife immediately, but the baby too had died. Oh, even now his fists clenched at the thought of that old woman scarring Ann's limp body.

Bill shook his head, trying to jerk himself back to the present. *Ann, you know I had to marry, had to have someone to raise Naomi and Jimmy. He was so little, just over a year old. Maybe that's what went wrong, maybe it was too soon after Jimmy to have another baby. But Nadine's had six and they've all come with no trouble at all. 'Course she was bigger than you Ann – well 'least-wise she was bigger when I married her. Now she's bent and scroney. She weaves like a drunk man when she's totin' a load.*

Although he had always believed her to be plain compared to Ann, Bill had convinced Nadine's father that he found his new wife perfectly lovely. He often made the comparison, looking fondly on the portrait of Ann that hung in the parlor next to his parents' portraits. But Nadine was good with the children and Naomi and Jimmy had attached themselves to her right away.

Bill had believed he could build the same life with Nadine that he'd enjoyed with Ann. He was a valuable man on the hog farms, able to turn a profit when all others failed. But after Ann's death, the swine sickened him. So, they moved up onto the plateau seeking a new start. He tried buying his own farm. Despite his success on the farm, the joy was short lived. So, he told Nadine he'd go look for work and be back to get the family shortly. That was the beginning and it must have been near fifteen years since he first wandered off the Cumberland Plateau to see if happiness awaited him in the surrounding valleys.

That creature called 'happiness' proved elusive and despite journeying further and further, he still found himself climbing back up this old mountain-road time and again. Now, as he heard the rush of Clear Creek he knew he was very near home. Shadows were growing long in the deep ravine as he stepped on the swinging bridge at the ferry crossing. He mapped the route in his mind up the steep hillside, through the nigh way to the Monterey Road then on to Campground where he'd left Nadine and the children in a rented house.

On the north side of the bridge, he met a local man and threw his head back in the customary greeting.

"Well, is that Bill Lewis? Don't know when I've seen you."

"Been travelin' a bit. You doing okay Andy?"

"Doin' fair I reckon. It's gettin' on toward suppertime; reckon you'll make it home in time?"

Bill shook his head confidently, "If the ole' woman doesn't have it on the table, she'll scare up somethin' for me. Always has b'fore."

With that, Bill nodded again at his neighbor and continued up the hill, glad to have had a moment's rest. As he walked, he nodded his head again, reassuring himself that Nadine would in fact be there to care for him, just as she always was.

Chapter 3

Bill Lewis had four boys and with the birth of each he'd thought he should be the proudest man in the county. In fact, when Jimmy was born eighteen years ago, he had beamed at his wife Ann and declared no one could be happier. Of course Jimmy didn't remember that moment. All he remembered was a Father that couldn't be pleased no matter what the child did; and Jimmy really did long for his father's approval although he could never have explained just why.

With his father gone more often than he was at home, Jimmy had naturally stepped into the father's role for his younger brothers. Jerry, just two years younger, sometimes balked at Jimmy's leadership, but ultimately, he knew that he didn't really want the responsibility of the whole family. So, that duty fell on young shoulders very early. No man in the community would have questioned that Jimmy Lewis was the head of that household and that he was man enough to fill the role.

Now Jimmy's mind began to turn toward his own life, separate from Bill and Nadine's family. The only sibling with whom he shared a mother, Naomi, had already left home.

Though he missed Naomi, he was actually thankful that he no longer had to fill that particular mouth. Anyway he knew that the Tyler family into which she'd married were hard working and successful; she would not go hungry living among them. Jimmy shook his head as that line of thought led him to pondering when Jerry might say vows to Vera Austin. Of course Jimmy couldn't let his younger brother beat him to marrying one of the Austin sisters. *How long will Pansy wait for me*, he asked himself.

Jimmy was abruptly jerked from his musings as Jerry, Lou and little Harry made their way into the hard-packed, dirt yard. Their faces and hands blended in with the dusty clothes and caused Jimmy to grin at them. He called to them as they came into shouting range, "Did you take a dirt bath today?"

Harry was grinning bigger than the rest. The youngest of the family, he tried to pull more than his seven year old share of the load. Today he was dragging a half filled sack, stopping every few steps to try to hoist it onto his back as his older brothers did. "Jimmy, wait till you see!"

Now Harry was trying to run, but the weight he was dragging held him back. Jimmy went out to meet him, scooping up both boy and sack. "Wha'cha got in there little 'un?"

Harry's white teeth stood out in contrast to the dirty brown face as he answered his big brother, "Taters!"

"What?" Jimmy looked to Jerry as he asked the question. "You were s'posed to work at the tater farm today, not steal from it."

Jerry took a step back from Jimmy who he knew from experience could still easily whip him. "Now you just hang on a minute there. We ain't stole nothun. We did a fair day's work only they didn't want to pay Harry. Weren't right though 'cause he picked up more taters than most of the bigger boys. So's the boss said he'd pay Harry in kind. 'Cept all the taters in these sacks are the culls. They were cut too bad to sell good."

Jimmy was liking what he was hearing now. He set Harry on the ground and tousled his hair. "Well now little'un, looks like you've fed the family for the next month. Mother can do all kinds of stuff with this many taters."

Harry shrugged his shoulders, seemingly brushing aside the praise he lived for. "All cut up though. Don't guess they'll keep too good."

Lou chuckled, feeling safe to enter the conversation for the first time. "Won't last long enough to rot 'round here."

Nodding his head, Jimmy was already leading Harry toward the rain barrel for a bit of washing. All of the boys knew better than to enter their mother's house carrying half the field with them. "We'll get you fit for Mother and let you tell her what you've brought her. Shore will make her happy, don't you think?"

Harry was grinning again, anxious to please his beloved mother.

All four boys knocked off as much dust as possible and scrubbed hands and face in the tepid rain water. Jimmy had Harry finished first and he went ahead and scrubbed a pan full of the precious potatoes. Harry's arms were filled with the pan as he entered his mother's kitchen. The smell of corn pone was already thick in the dark little room.

Nadine Lewis stooped near the low fireplace adjusting the coals atop her makeshift Dutch oven. "I heard you boys a long time ago, thought you never would make it inside."

As she turned to greet them, she immediately saw Harry's burden. Her first thought was to scold the older boys for making him carry the load when their hands were empty, but she checked her words as she saw the joy in her youngest son's eyes. "Harry, what's that?"

"Tater's Mother! I earned them today. An' there's lots more outside. I reckon I'll put 'em in a big basket and set 'em somewhere's cool."

Nadine did not entirely understand, although she was accustomed to her boys coming home with food for the table. She just never knew quite what it would be. And she was always cautioning them that they must come by these things honestly. Somehow though, she couldn't bring herself to question Jimmy too often. She was sure that he showed up with too many chickens when Jerry could only kill squirrels or rabbits. With each boy she tried all the harder to impress the Bible's code of honesty. Perhaps she had not started this work early enough with Jimmy.

In the early years, the lesson hadn't been so pertinent. Bill moved them constantly and seldom stayed with a single job for very long, but at least there was food. Then, as his wanderings grew longer and longer, she had to rely on Jimmy to feed them. Now even little Harry was pitching in. She squeezed the boy in her arms and bit back a tear as she realized he should have been in school today instead of working in the fields.

"Tomorrow, young man, you must go to school with your sisters. You'll never learn to read and write out there stooped over a potato row."

"Can't eat writin' Mother."

"Maybe not now Harry, but someday being able to read and write will put food in your stomach."

Harry did not see that logic and responded only with his characteristic shrug. It was hard for him to think of sending his brothers to work while he flopped in the school room. Surely school was for girls.

Chapter 4

Nadine Lewis set the piping hot pone of cornbread on the rough board table beside boiled potatoes and cooked cabbage. Her girls were already taking their seats as she called for the boys to gather for their evening meal.

"Wow, we've got potatoes *and* cabbage tonight?" questioned Mary. It seemed like a holiday feast for she was accustomed to only seeing one dish on the supper table, and often that dish was far too small to feed all seven children.

Nadine smiled at her youngest daughter and breathed a quiet prayer of thanksgiving that she was able to please her with this simple meal.

The boys were quickly seating themselves as Nadine explained to Mary, "Your little brother did such a good day's work that he was rewarded with nearly a bushel of potatoes." She stooped to kiss the top of Harry's head as she passed him going to the water bucket.

Nadine longed to put milk on the table for she knew her children desperately needed it. But, they rarely had fresh milk unless a kind neighbor saw fit to share with them. She knew, however, that it would not be missed with tonight's meal.

"Quiet now, we need to return thanks for this meal," this was the only time Nadine ever raised her voice to her family.

The room was immediately silent as Nadine bowed her head over her children and prayed, "Father God, we thank Thee for these bountiful blessings we are enjoying tonight. Thank You Lord for good work the boys have enjoyed and we pray Your blessings on the farmers who sent the potatoes. In the name of Jesus we pray, Amen."

It took only a moment for glasses to be filled with water, for the bowls of food to be passed and then silence returned as each child greedily ate their meal. Nadine rarely sat at the table for she always waited and ate only the food that the children left. Many meals, there were only crumbs left but she could never go to bed with her own belly full when her children were still hungry. Tonight, however, there was plenty and she took her chair at the end of the table.

Nadine had very nearly cleared her plate and the older children were working on their second helpings when the front door burst open.

"By-jingo, it's as quiet as a cemetery here. Have y'uns all died off?" Bill Lewis' sudden appearance in the doorway so shocked his family that forks were frozen in mid-air and mouths were agape.

"Bill," Nadine whispered. Shaking her head slightly, she quickly pulled her thoughts together enough to respond to her husband. "Bill, you're in time for supper. I do hope there's enough left."

As she rose to bring another plate, Lou's hand shot out to the corn pone and quickly dragged a piece of bread under the table.

Nadine continued to talk, trying to incorporate Bill into the evening. "We were all busy eating I guess and weren't saying too much. Didn't realize we were all that quiet though. Here, sit right down here in your place, children pass the food bowls to your father."

Bill walked through the front room knocking dirt from his long coat and brushing at his dusty pants. Roberta rolled her eyes at Winnie silently noting that their clean floor would need more work before bedtime.

"Well, I am starving. Been walking a right smart piece and that sure works up an appetite."

Jimmy couldn't help questioning his father, "Walking? You had a fine horse when you left here three months ago. Why weren't you ridin'?"

"Ah, he weren't no good a'tall. I left him in Knoxville and rode the train as fur as Harriman."

Jimmy grinned, reading between the lines of his father's story. "Harriman? Train comes all the way to Monterey now you know. That would have been a much nicer walk and you wouldn't have had to climb the mountain."

Bill ignored his grown son's mocking. "By-jingo, Harriman's as fur as I rode. Din' ride no further. Now, what's this we're eatin'? Taters and... is that cabbage? Ain't ya got no side meat fried?"

"No Bill, but here's some cornbread, I even think it's still warm," Nadine explained.

"Guess y'uns ate all the side meat already."

Jerry was happy to set his father straight. "No Sir, we ain't had side meat since Mr. MacDonald killed his last hog. He brought us a goodly chunk at that time and some fat too that the girls rendered into lard."

"Ole' man MacDonald been bringing you charity?" Bill growled despite his overly full mouth of potatoes and bread.

"Nadee," Bill always chose to drop the final syllable of his wife's name. "At least bring me some buttermilk. A man can't eat bread and water, why, that's what they feed you in prison."

Nadine looked at the floor as she responded to him, "There's no buttermilk on the place Bill, nor sweet milk neither. We all drank water tonight."

Again Jerry wanted to fill in the details, "We've been drinking water for over a week. That was the last time Mrs. Edwards come bringing a pail of milk for us."

Bill shook his head in frustration that the menu did not suit him. He chose to ignore his son's pointed remarks. "Tomorrow I'll want meat on the table."

Jimmy mumbled under his breath as he walked out the back door, "Then you'll have to put it on the table."

With his stomach filled, Bill stood announcing, "Well, I'm plumb wore out. I'll have to get on to bed."

As he left the table, each child stood to complete their evening chores without any prompting from their mother. The girls knew the floor would have to be swept again, Jerry steered Harry out the back door with water buckets and they could already hear Jimmy's axe ringing out his annoyance on the firewood.

Gradually, the family banter returned and the children finished their evening as normally as possible. Nadine saw each one to bed, reminding them to wash face, hands and feet before lying down on their straw ticks. None of them had shoes and she was intent that the day's dirt not go to bed with them. She kissed each freshly scrubbed cheek and silently prayed over each child in turn. Returning to the kitchen, she carried three pairs of dirty overalls and Mary's dress. As she scrubbed out the clothes in the kitchen, she inspected the patches on the youngest children's clothes. These garments had been passed down several times and were now a maze of patches. Tonight it seemed she could wash them without re-patching anything. She hung each item close to the fire and added an extra log, thankful that the big old fireplace would have them dried by morning. Lou, Mary and Harry now had only one set of clothes each and Jerry's best clothes now needed patches so she washed at night while the children slept.

Nadine was up again at dawn, with dark hollows about her eyes that testified the fact that this was a routine schedule for her. Bill was up shortly after her and found her stirring the fire for breakfast.

"Have you got the coffee goin' yet?" He asked.

"There isn't any coffee, Bill. I'll have some cornmeal mush cookin' in just a few minutes. And we do have some eggs. I could fry you some of the mush if you want to wait till it sets."

The only response Nadine heard was, "Mush?" The remainder of Bill's monologue was so mumbled she couldn't make it out and she was pretty sure she was happy to have missed it.

"How long you let them kids sleep? They won't make their fortune a'layin in bed you know." Loudly he called, "Git on up now, there's work to be done."

Turning to Nadine he announced, "This ain't no way to live. I'll head out and get us a proper livin' started today."

Chapter 5

Morning dawned cold especially in the old house's loft bedroom. As his eyes blinked awake, Harry's first question was to his brother, "Jerry, din' you bank that far?" All four brothers had only one bed to share. However, Jimmy had recently given up and begun sleeping on the floor. The fireplace warmed the floor during the daytime but even the addition of a big hardwood log at night rarely ensured more than a good bed of coals in the morning and no noticeable heat.

"You think you're cold? Least you got a straw tick under ya'. These ole' boards are like ice this mornin'." Jimmy was out of his blankets in a flash and pulling on his thickest shirt before Harry and Lou could even get out of the bed.

From the other side of the blanket-wall they could hear their sisters already stirring.

It was only minutes before all of the children were downstairs, huddling close to the fire their mother had already nursed from the night's coals. She had the water bucket sitting near the flame to thaw the thin sheet of ice on its top and they could already see the preparations for their cornmeal mush.

Nadine greeted her family with a warm smile and hugs for Mary and Harry. "Harry, get your overalls on; those bare legs are going to give you a chill. The clothes are all nice and dry after being by the fire all night."

Father entered the room already dressed in boots that he'd made shine like the river at midnight. He was carrying his long duster-coat. "Nadee, you reckon you can knock the dust off this ole' coat? By-jingo, can't go 'round lookin' like a pauper or you'll always be one." He surveyed his sons, barefoot and clad in patched overalls and ragged shirts. "You boys'd do well to remember that yerselves."

Jimmy and Jerry looked at each other and back at their father in disgust. Bill was unaffected by their scorn.

"Where are you boys off to today? Yesterday, it looked like the fencing around that barn needed some attention. Maybe that's what you ought to work on today."

As usual, Jimmy spoke on behalf of the family, "We've still got work to do at the Tater Farm and that pays wages. So that's where we'll all be goin' today."

"That's well and good for you and Jerry, but Lou, have you finished your schoolin'?"

Lou stepped forward to answer his father. The thirteen year old boy was torn between the loathing he sensed from his brothers and a sincere fear of this man who exerted such influence whenever he was home. "Well Sir, I finished the second primer book an' I can count and do sums."

Bill nodded his head, "As good as I could expect. You go on with your brothers to the fields. Harry, you will go with the girls to school. I'll not have any stupid boys carryin' the Lewis name."

Harry started to protest but his mother's hand held him firmly by the shoulder and he knew he could not ignore her wishes.

Satisfied that he had his family organized for the day, Bill announced his own plans. "I'm going out to get a start today at our fortune. This here is no way to live."

Mother had served the cornmeal mush in tin bowls to each child, her husband and herself. Roberta had placed a mug of water in front of each bowl.

"What are ya' thinkin' you'll do?" Jerry boldly questioned his father.

"Don't rightly know. Something always turns up though, don't it?"

The simple meal was quickly finished and the older boys left on the long walk to Woody for their work day. The girls, along with Harry, set about the morning's house chores with very little direction from their mother. And Bill strode out the door holding himself as though he were a wealthy gentleman.

The evening brought the family back together again. Nadine had prepared a duplicate of yesterday's meal with the welcome addition of fresh milk delivered by a kind neighbor. She was just thinking that the children would be pleased when she heard her husband coming through the front door calling and complaining in the same breath.

"What's that awful smell? Surely we're not eating cabbage a second day in a row? Nadee! Did you not even cook; is that the supper we had last night."

Nadine couldn't help but wring her hands, "Now Bill, of course I've cooked it fresh. But yes, it's pretty much the same. We do have milk tonight though."

"Milk? By-jingo a man can't live on cabbage and milk." He tossed a slab of meat on the table, scattering tin plates and forks. "Fry me up some meat. We'll be eatin' now. I've bought a store today."

Nadine looked from his face to the meat lying on her clean table and back again to her husband. "What? A store? Where? How?"

The questions came all out of order, but her mind seemed out of order at the moment.

"It's over in Cliff Springs. I think it'll be a good business, if I can get these young'uns to work."

"Bill, they are good workers, every one of them. Why, little Mary will go out and work in the fields the same as the boys, and Roberta and Winnie keep as good a house as I can ever hope to." Nadine moved to slice the meat and raked coals from the fireplace to heat her heavy skillet.

She sliced thick chunks for Bill and continued slicing enough for each of the children to have a small helping. She wasn't sure if that had been her husband's intention, but she certainly wanted to take the opportunity to feed her family meat any time she could.

Bill settled himself in a chair with his feet propped to warm by the fire. "We'll start packin' first thing in the morning. I'll have to go see the landlord 'bout this place, but them boys can load the house plunder in the wagon."

"Bill, don't you remember that we don't have anything to pull the wagon with. You traded the mules for that saddle horse right before you left last time."

"By-jingo, I b'lieve you're right. Well, I'll just have to bring a team back with me. Guess I'll have to walk out though. Awful tiresome a'walkin' ever-whir'."

The girls and Harry returned from school very shortly after their father. Harry immediately went out to feed his chickens and Mary followed with a basket hoping to find another egg. Only Roberta and Winnie stepped into the house in time to hear the end of their parents' conversation.

"Where are we going?" Winnie questioned her mother.

"Cliff Springs dear. Your father has bought a store there."

Winnie's face fell and she reached a slim hand out to steady herself on the dry sink. "What?" She was nearly shrieking. "I can't leave my friends and school and what about Roberta? She's teaching half of the class, what will they ever do without her?" By the time she finished spilling all of her questions, great tears were streaming down her face.

Bill showed no sympathy for his daughter's pain. "Stop that bellerin'! There's a school at Cliff Springs. I reckon they can teach you to read and cypher as well as Campground can. Anyhow, Cliff Springs is much more important a place than Campground – why, they had a post office for more'n fifteen year; prob'ly they'd still have one 'cept for some political maneuvering."

Winnie buried her face in her mother's shoulder, "He doesn't understand. He doesn't even care."

Such was the scene that greeted Jimmy, Jerry and Lou as they returned home. Jimmy took one look at his wailing sister and immediately turned questioning eyes to his father.

Bill ignored their unspoken demands as well as the dramatic scene his daughter was causing. "Nadee, you got that meat fried up yet? I'm a'starvin. We got a busy day ahead tomorrow so we'll all get to bed early. Boys, first thing tomorrow you'll need to load up all of the house plunder on that ole' wagon. We're movin' to Cliff Springs."

Bill silenced the boys protests that their work on the potato farm would be out of range, heaped his plate with the meat and potatoes and ate as he continued planning and directing the following day's work for each member of his family.

Chapter 6

None of the Lewises had ever visited Cliff Springs, although it lay only a few miles from Muddy Pond where they often attended revival meetings and where several of the children had friends. While packing, Nadine had pondered aloud whether she could have ridden through the community when she and Bill first came to live on the mountain.

"You know, we went back to Sand Springs when my sister died. God rest her soul, Opal was only twenty-three and left two little babies behind. How I longed to wrap them babies up and care for them like my very own. Opal was my only sister, you know. Roberta was a toddler then, it was before I had Lou. But of course we already had Naomi, Jimmy and Jerry and I never even asked 'cause I knew Bill wouldn't hear of takin' in another family."

Nadine rarely reminisced about her siblings or her childhood and both Roberta and Winnie enjoyed hearing even this sad story. Winne watched her mother as she carefully placed the pewter dishes in a wooden crate, treating them as though they were bone china. She saw a sadness pass across her mother's face as she talked about her sister, but it was gone in an instant as Mother turned her thoughts to her children and the home she would have to create in this new place. None of the children had fond feelings for their father this day and hearing even a hint of sadness from Mother fueled a spark of bitterness that sprang to life in their young hearts when told they'd have to leave everything they knew to chase Father's mysterious fortune.

The heat of the day bore down on the family as they placed the last of their belongings in the rickety wagon and ten sets of eyes turned east toward their new home.

The drive took them across a nearly-dry creek and up the steep mountain beyond it. The road was paved with sharp stones that cut at bare feet, for the children had to follow the wagon most of the way to spare the horses. As they passed beyond Muddy Pond Baptist Church, Harry climbed upon the wagon and reached for Mother's hand. It was as far from Campground as he'd ever traveled. Even Mary stepped closer to Lou, asking a question so he wouldn't know that she was scared.

"Lou, you've been all over haven't you?"

"Reckon I've been 'bout ever'where," he smiled down at his younger sister as his mountain accent drawled 'where' like the whir of a pinwheel.

"You been to Cliff Springs?"

Lou disliked being forced to confess he had not seen quite every community on the mountain, much less all points on the Earth. "Nope, never made it to Cliff Springs before."

Mary kept her eyes on the road as the quickly fading light cast eerie shadows from the tall oaks surrounding them. Even though her brother had never seen this new home, she trusted he'd still know all about it. "You think there'll be children to play with when we get there?"

He smiled, relieved that Mary's concerns were no heavier than the availability of playmates. Lou was more concerned with a roof that didn't leak too much and wood to cook a bite of food. He heard Jimmy and Jerry talking and he worried with them that they'd be all on their own to find food for the family.

The child's concerns actually served to lighten the burden he had carried up the mountain and he reached to pick Mary up.

"Children will come from miles around just to play with you, Mary." He rubbed the back of her neck with his nose eliciting squeals from the comforted girl.

All chatter ceased as the sun set and the last couple of miles were carefully picked along a road that in places was no more than a stock path. Finally, Bill pulled the team to a halt before a worn cabin. There were no lights inside, nor could any be seen either up or down the road.

"Whoa girls," Bill spoke gently to his horses. "Been a long day for you I know, we'll get them bits outta your mouths right away." Without turning his head, he began calling orders to his sons. "Jimmy, get this team unhitched and rubbed down. You gotta take care of your stock you know – good book says so. Jimmy, start unloadin' this wagon."

Nadine gently laid her hand on his arm and asked, "We've loaded the bedding right at the back of the wagon. Maybe we should just make pallets on the porch and do the moving in daylight?"

"Hmmf," Bill grunted his consent. "Get them horses cared for."

He jumped from the wagon and walked slowly away as though he were assessing the property even in the darkness.

All of the family worked through their exhaustion to pull the worn quilts from the wagon and spread them haphazardly on the porch. Lou thought to himself as he fell beside Harry, *I hope this is the right house. Sure would hate to have some farmer come trip over us going to milk his cow in the morning."*

Chapter 7

As the family rose and gathered their blankets to start a long day, they were all shocked by the ramshackle condition of their new home, considering it was part of the property Bill Lewis purchased with the Cliff Springs General Store.

Bill immediately headed for the store building. Roberta caught Jimmy's eye as he glowered at his father's back; they watched as he ambled across the store's front porch looking in the windows and down the road then made his way to the back door and disappeared inside. Convinced they would receive no help from him settling into the ramshackle house, Roberta turned to join her family as they unloaded the wagon.

As things began to come to order inside the house, Roberta stepped outside with the homemade broom in one hand, wiping her brow with the other. The sun beat down on her as she began to sweep the hard packed dirt that made up the front yard of the little house. *Why doesn't Father ever move us into a house with pretty green grass?* Her thoughts propelled the broom faster and harder as every leaf and pebble gave way clearing the space as neatly as the interior floors were kept.

Roberta had already scrubbed the floor in the house's front room, although she failed to understand why Mother insisted on such cleanliness. After all, it was not as though they ever invited visitors – unless you could count the ruffians that Father often invited in for supper, scarce though their own food was. In fact, her oldest sister, Naomi, had married Tim Tyler without his family ever seeing the inside of their last rented home. The Tylers had hosted all of the Lewises at their simple but spacious farm house – well all of them except Father who hadn't been home at the time.

Now Father had found yet another broken down house for them to live in and this time it was located miles from all of their friends. At least in Campground the neighbors were kind to them and would help Mother as they could but here in Cliff Springs they didn't know a soul. Yet, Father was convinced this store he'd bought would be the key to his fortune and his happiness.

Roberta didn't understand why happiness seemed such an elusive creature for her father. Mother had nothing but her family and she worked her fingers to the bone. Yet she would walk in the fields and pick wildflowers with her daughters smiling and breathing deeply of the fresh mountain air; and she was always laughing as her sons played games with sticks and rocks. She seemed to be happy and Roberta wondered what was different with her father.

Father! Again her thoughts pushed the broom. *Fortune. Why are you always seeking a fortune? Why don't you just find a steady job? Why can't you find joy in this family?*

Roberta kept her thoughts to herself. Mother would not hear the children saying one word against their father. But Roberta couldn't help but wonder if Mother would say some of these things directly to the man maybe their life would not be so difficult? She looked at her feet, filthy from the dusty yard and remembered Father wiping off shiny black boots before he walked the few yards to the store this morning. Mother had brushed his long duster-coat and revealed a lovely camel's hair fabric – Roberta looked down at her patched cotton dress and felt she would surely scream out loud.

Instead, Roberta Lewis gave her head a swift shake and pulled her mind from the self-pitying that she despised. *You won't get anywhere feeling sorry for yourself. Just have to focus on pulling yourself up out of this. There is a better life; people all around us are living it. For the time being, you just have to help Mother and do as she asks you.*

As she entered the little parlor room Roberta noted that Mother had already hung the family's most prized possessions. Three large portraits, clad in gilded frames, now graced the walls. Grandma and Grandpa Lewis scowled down from the south wall and Ann Lewis solemnly stared from the east wall. Naomi and Jimmy were always happy to have their mother's portrait hanging in the parlor but Roberta felt it somehow morbid. No one here remembered Ann Lewis except their father.

A loud crash in the kitchen sent Roberta rushing from the parlor.

"Could somebody come in here and help me," Jimmy was yelling as he balanced a stove pipe on one shoulder and tried to fit another section into the bottom of it.

"What are you doing Jimmy? There is black soot all over this floor!" Even as she fussed, Roberta rushed to grab the pipe from his shoulders and allow him the freedom of movement he'd need to connect the pipes.

"Mother is so excited to have this rickety ole' stove that was left here, so I wanted to get it workin'. But it won't do no good if'n it's not got a stove pipe." With a slight grunt he pushed the pieces together and lifted the final section from Roberta's arms into the wall.

"There. Now, do you want to clean the floor or build the fire? Don't know if this thing'll draw or just smoke up the whole place."

Roberta smiled at her brother who always seemed to expect the worst. "You build the fire, I'll get the broom."

As Jimmy returned with a hand full of pine cones and little sticks, he was already thinking of his next chore. "There's broken planks on the back porch, I know one of y'uns will fall through it. But I guess I'd better see to patching the roof first – when I carried the blankets upstairs, I could see daylight through the ceiling."

There were plenty of chores for the whole family as they tried to make the house livable. For days they worked and each day Bill Lewis went into his new store. The evenings brought him home with one complaint after another. He complained about the meals Nadine cooked; he complained about the condition of the house and the condition of the store.

With each new complaint, Jimmy and Jerry just looked at each other. They were getting bolder each day in their communication with their father. A confrontation seemed imminent.

The people of the Cliff Springs community had all come out to greet the new store keeper. Some of the women even ventured by to say hello to his family. The supper table revealed offerings from some of the neighbors – a bowl of turnip greens, a shoofly pie and jars of homemade jam.

Roberta had noticed that the women discreetly looked around their home, no doubt noting the absence of upholstered furnishings or cut glass lamps. Each caller told how they looked forward to doing business with the Lewis family. It seemed that Bill Lewis was a natural-born merchant; he could talk to anyone and convince a shopper to buy twice what he came for. He could calm any complaints and the customers always left with a smile on their face.

Bill Lewis seemed to be a completely different man when he was tending store than when he was at home.

Chapter 8

"Well, they're sure smiling when they come out the door," Jerry commented.

Lou swung his feet over the porch rail on which he was propped, "Guess he's a fine store keeper. Look at all them packages they're carryin'."

Harry made a loud spewing sound as he attempted to spit off the porch. He'd been practicing spitting like his big brothers all afternoon. It was a rare day these boys spent lounging on a porch rail and the youngest was not about to waste the time. "Reckon what's wrapped up in them papers?"

Jimmy laughed and tousled little Harry's hair. "Well you've seen inside that store. Everything that's on the shelves and around the walls, that's what the folks are buying. What I can't figure out is why they buy it from him."

Winnie quietly answered Jimmy's question. "That's not hard to see, where else would they go? Nobody's gonna' drive to Monterey if the same goods can be had right here in Cliff Springs. Anyway, they come to the post office that the timber boss keeps so it's just easy to walk a little piece and get what they need from the store."

Winnie was making a very valid point. Cliff Springs boasted one small coal mine and one large tract of timber. As she sat in the porch swing, she had a ready view of the big three story home where the Philips lived. Members of that family owned both the mine and the timber. The men who worked both enterprises could hardly make the twenty mile round-trip to the nearest town when they had needs, and money to fill them.

Lou saw things differently. "Well, if'n I had a team, I'd sure go to Monterey ever' chance I got. There's everything in the world goin' on there – trains a comin' and a goin'. And big hotels with people from all over stayin' there."

Jimmy grinned at his brother, "Well, there's a fine team in the barn out there. Didn't you notice them when your father sent you out to feed last night?"

"That's just what I ought'ta do, go hitch up that long buckboard and take a lil' trip to town."

Jerry playfully punched Lou's shoulder as he warned, "You know if you touched one of those horses, he'd skin you alive. And Mother doesn't want us to cross him."

Jimmy slid off the rail and ambled toward the store building.

"What's buggin' him?" Winnie asked.

"Didn't you pay attention at breakfast? He was told to get the feed re-stacked today. Anyways, he don't like to hear about the stuff that's around here but we can't use," Jerry answered for him.

Jimmy slipped into the small side door to enter the store's tiny feed room. Stacked about him were brightly colored cotton sacks that held all manner of feeds for both human and animals. There were a few barrels holding other foodstuffs and several more dirty-white sacks with fertilizer and lower-grade hog and cattle feeds.

As he looked around, Jimmy could hear his father working behind the store's big counter. His skill was evident as he chatted with the customers.

"Here you are Ma'am. That calico fabric will sure look pretty on one of your girls."

"Oh, Mr. Lewis, I was splurging for a new dress for myself."

"Ah, well it will be all the lovelier on you, of course. Don't you need some lace to go on the collar?"

"Well, I hadn't thought of adding lace, but that really would give it a whole different look…"

How does he go on like that? Jimmy wondered as he tried to turn his attention to the work he'd been assigned.

He may sound ridiculous to me, but I've got to admit, he's making money here. And we may never see a red penny of it, but at least there is food on the table good and regular. And at least Mother isn't always worrying and walking the hills looking for any kind of wild vegetable she can feed us.

The more Jimmy thought about his father, the faster the heavy bags moved. It was hard to give the man any credit for success when the whole family was just waiting for him to leave again – for they were certain he would be leaving again.

Jimmy tried to count how many months Bill Lewis had been home with his family. It had been enough months to get the rickety old house livable, for Mother to plant a big garden and even for the girls to make some new friends.

Hearing the movement in the feed room, Bill joined his oldest son announcing, "I've got to go to the depot in Monterey to pick up a supply order. Do you think you can do the numbers well enough to keep the store until I get back?"

Something inside Jimmy leaped at the thought of his father giving him such responsibility. And yet, there were years and layers of resentment that dispelled the moment's pride. His answer was as surly as he usually responded to his father.

"Don't see no reason why I couldn't. You know sums come pretty natural to me."

Bill seemed satisfied with the answer, "Well when you are finished in here, come on out to the store and I'll show you some things." Before he left the room, he looked his son over from head to toe, "Don't think you can wear them overalls though. Wear your better ones tomorrow."

Jimmy just shook his head as his father closed the door and he was silently ranting at the man when Roberta joined him.

"What's the matter Jimmy? You look fit to be tied."

Pointing at the door Jimmy explained, "He comes in here and tells me tomorrow I should wear my better overalls. Don't he know that the only other pair I've got have bigger patches than these?"

"Why's he want you to look good tomorrow?"

"I'm going to keep the store." A little bit of the pride returned and he puffed his chest out ever-so-slightly.

Roberta was shocked. "Why?"

"He's going to Monterey to pick up a load of supplies."

"Hmmf. How many months do you reckon it'll take him to get a wagon home from Monterey?" Roberta left, having completely forgotten what message or errand brought her to the store room in the first place.

With the sacks neatly stacked and the barrels lined up, Jimmy was turning toward the store when Roberta burst back through the door. "Jimmy! I have an idea."

"Well do you reckon the idea is as big as your eyes are right now?"

"Jimmy, I'm serious. If he wants his kids looking a little better, we'll just start working on that while he's gone tomorrow. I'm going to get enough dress goods to make Winnie a new dress. And if he don't come back tomorrow night then I'll get enough for Mary. By the time he gets home, I may be able to have all of us looking like a proper merchant's family."

"And if he catches you, we'll both get skinned. But I think that's a great idea."

At sunrise, Bill Lewis was rousing Jerry and Lou to harness the team and hitch the wagon.

Lou took the opportunity to mention that he'd just yesterday been dreaming about a trip to town. His father responded, "I don't have time for young'uns to be following me around."

Lou thought about arguing that he could help load the supplies and that he wouldn't slow him down at all. But he thought better of it, knowing there would be no invitation to ride along and no explanation why.

As Jimmy started down the steep stairs, he heard movement from his sisters' room and knew that Roberta would be following him to the store as soon as their father's wagon was out of sight.

The trip could have been made in a day of hard driving. But no one expected Bill Lewis to drive his fine new team too hard, nor push himself too much. So Roberta had no trouble finishing Winnie's dress.

The next morning she brought Winnie into the kitchen for Mother's inspection. Nadine was utterly shocked. "Wherever did you get that fabric?"

"From the store of course," was Roberta's frank reply.

"Roberta Lewis, have you stolen from your own father?"

"Mother!" Her voice was sharper than she'd ever spoken to her mother. "How can you call it stealing when his children are in rags? Why, he even told Jimmy that he needed to wear better overalls while he was keeping store."

Nadine's voice was calm despite her daughter's rebuke. "Roberta, you must always respect your father. The Bible commands it, you know."

Roberta bowed her head. She knew her mother was right about respecting her father. "But it's so hard to respect that man when he does nothing for us."

Nadine began to list her husband's best features and she was pointing out the blessings they were currently enjoying when the rest of the children began to filter into the kitchen.

Jimmy quickly understood the nature of the lecture. "Mother, I don't want to disrespect you, but if he don't come back for months this time, I think we've got a good trade here at the store and we can manage just fine without him."

The look on Nadine's face expressed her disapproval of his sentiments.

Jerry joined in, agreeing with his brother. Roberta continued to fuss over Winnie's dress and Winnie was so thrilled to have something new that she could speak nothing but praises for Roberta.

By the time breakfast was finished and the family began to disperse for their day's chores, Nadine Lewis was thoroughly frustrated and saddened. As the older boys walked out the door she could hear them continue to criticize their father. In fact, they could hardly call him 'Father'. She began to see her husband reflected in her children.

Alone for a moment in the suddenly-silent kitchen, she whispered, "Ye are of your father the devil..." And she bowed her head in silent prayer.

Chapter 9

Roberta sat on a split-bottom chair, enjoying a rare July breeze, while she hemmed her new dress. On the pale pink calico she had carefully embroidered rosebuds around the collar and the cuffs of the sleeves. With just a few more stitches, she would have the first new dress she'd owned in – well, she wasn't sure she could remember another brand new dress. She was always just thrilled to get Naomi's hand-me-downs. She smiled at the thought, remembering that she'd grown a few inches taller than Naomi so she was always struggling to let down hems.

Roberta straightened her back and shook out the garment as Nadine Lewis stepped onto the porch, a big pan of green beans resting in the bend of her arm.

"Oh Mother, don't you think it's just beautiful? Have you ever seen a sweeter fabric?"

Nadine looked at the dress and at her daughter's beautiful smile. She secretly felt that Roberta was the prettiest of her own three girls. Even her step-daughter Naomi was a beautiful lady now but somehow Roberta's vibrant smile shone over her too. She thought how many times over the years Bill had remarked on the similarity of Naomi and her mother Ann. He believed his first wife was the most beautiful women he'd ever seen. Nadine wondered if he could even see the beauty in any of his daughters.

Smiling at her daughter, Nadine moved closely to inspect the needlework. "Roberta, you are a wonder with a needle. That embroidery could be in a city dress shop."

Roberta beamed. She had worked very hard first on Winnie's dress and now her own. "Well, it's all finished. I need to turn to on the blue fabric I brought over for Mary."

"Roberta, your father will be ill with all of us if he finds out you've taken fabric from the store."

They had discussed this many times over the three days since Bill Lewis left to buy supplies in Monterey. Roberta had no desire to worry her mother. "Well, we just won't let him know, now will we? I don't think he ever notices any of us. Do you think he'd know whether we were wearing a burlap sack or a silk ball gown?"

Mother and daughter shared a laugh as they stepped into the house. "I'll be happy to have a dress for Mary to wear to school. I guess the Cliff Springs school will start in just a few weeks, don't you think?"

Nadine looked to the calendar she'd tacked on the kitchen wall and was shocked to realize it was nearly August. "Yes, I suppose it will start soon. You will go with the younger ones, won't you?"

Roberta shrugged her shoulders, "Guess so. I'll be the oldest one in the building 'cept the teacher. But I know I still have a lot to learn. My ciphers are very weak."

"Dear, you are so sweet and beautiful that no one will ever care whether you can even count."

"But Mother, I need to be able to take care of myself. Just think, maybe I could help a shop keeper someday. Wouldn't that be so much better than the field work that, uh…"

Nadine smiled as she heard her daughter stumble over her words, trying not to offend her mother. "The field work that I have to do? Yes, Roberta, I don't want any of my girls to have to be out in the fields, scavenging for wild greens and berries."

It was the closest thing to complaining that Roberta had ever heard from her mother.

Jimmy effectively ended their talk as he stepped into the kitchen. Each day since Father left, he was in the store bright and early and left only for a half hour lunch. The customers had not slowed with his care and Nadine thought he'd found work that he would truly enjoy.

"How has the morning gone, Jimmy?" Nadine asked him.

"I reckon it's been good. Busy. Only my stomach reminded me it was time to shut the door for a few minutes."

Nadine left the beans she'd begun breaking and cut off a big slice of bread, brought pickles to the table and cheese. Without being asked, Roberta stirred coals in the little cookstove and prepared to fry meat for him. Accustomed to watching for their father to come to the house for the noon meal, the children took their cue from Jimmy and quickly filtered in and seated themselves.

"Harry, Roberta and I were just talking about school. It will be starting up soon and I'm so happy you will be able to go from day one since you aren't needed on the potato farm this year."

Harry scowled, "Pro'bly they need me, but it's just we can't git there from here. Anyhow, don't Jimmy and Jerry need my help instead of me wasting my time in a schoolroom?"

"Harry, it will not be a waste. You are nine years old now and you ought to be reading more than you are. Maybe you should read with me some here at home to get ready to go back?"

"Don't have time." Harry declared with an air of finality.

Nadine did not argue with her son. Surely Bill would be here to encourage him to go. Bill understood their need for education.

Jerry looked to Jimmy, once again the head of their household. "Jimmy, we gonna stay here if Father doesn't come home? Don't you reckon we should go back to Campground before the winter?"

Nadine looked shocked, but waited for Jimmy to answer the question.

"Don't know how we'd go back. We've got no money to get a place. Father took all of the money with him, except for what I've collected these past few days. Anyhow, we do have the store here."

Nadine appreciated the answer and wanted to support it, "Well, of course you'll keep running the store until your father gets home. He'll be here anytime now."

Jimmy wasn't quite as positive as she was, "We are running very low on some of the stock. If he doesn't get back with the supplies, we can't keep the store open all winter. I didn't realize how many things we were nearly out of until I was the one to fill orders."

Roberta had learned quickly that access to the store could be a blessing to the family, even without any money. "But there are foodstuffs there. Even if we had to shut the doors, we would be able to make it through the winter, wouldn't we?"

"Well of course we'll make it through the winter," Nadine encouraged. We've got lots of beans to be picked and dried. And there are potatoes in the garden and there's an apple tree out behind the store that we'll harvest. So, we'll hear no more about whether we'll survive."

The children all settled to their lunch and did not again mention their concerns. Nadine was thankful that she didn't have to face them again, when Bill arrived by noon on the fourth day.

He rolled in with the wagon piled high with supplies. And four pink piglets corralled in a little pen at the front of it all.

Everyone was about their chores when he arrived and began summoning his children with work for each of them. They were all thrilled and surprised to see the little pigs. "What will we do with them?" "Are they for us?" they pelted their father with questions.

"We'll fatten them and ought to be able to slaughter them before the weather gets too warm in the spring. Jerry and Lou, you'll have to keep them slopped. You go right now and make sure we've got a pen to keep them in. If they get off in the woods, we may lose them since they've just been weaned from their mother."

Bill turned his head from side to side, "Where's Jimmy? Has he run off all the customers since I've been gone?" He raised his voice, "Jimmy," he yelled.

Jimmy stepped out of the store and began answering his father's questions.

Nadine also heard his calls and quickly came out to greet her husband with a bright smile. But he was only interested in the store.

Bill was happy to be home and happier still that his thriving business had not suffered from his absence.

Chapter 10

The winter of 1925 proved extremely cold. It snowed and snowed and the Lewis family moved from huddling at the fireplace to huddling in the kitchen at mealtimes. The boys had worked hard to seal the little house but thin walls, gaps in the roofing and inadequate clothing plagued them throughout the cold months.

Still, each day, Bill sent Jerry or Lou to the store early in the morning to fire the potbellied stove. Harry was sent out to tend the hogs which were fattening nicely on the corn shocks they had lashed against the side of the barn. Some mornings, Harry felt the barn might actually be warmer than his bed.

When the weather allowed, the five youngest children walked to the little one room schoolhouse. Roberta was in fact the oldest student but still somewhat behind many of the younger ones since she had not had access to the school books many of them had enjoyed. Most of the children came from miners or loggers' homes but somehow these children had been given more than the prosperous storekeeper's family. And this fact was not lost on the Lewis children. However, each evening Harry and Mary were wrapped in their mother's arms and applauded for their work in school that day. Harry's resistance to school melted as Nadine praised the letters he formed on his slate each evening. He read from the battered McGuffey's Primer and smiled proudly as first sentences and then stories emerged.

Each evening Bill came home after he closed the doors to the store and complained of the cold he'd faced as he walked the few yards from store building to house. Nadine always had his supper waiting with the children clean and ready to take their place at the table. Bill complained about the food that she cooked while the children rejoiced in it.

At the first of February, with no end of the severe weather in sight, Bill declared the hogs were topped out nicely. He seemed to praise the animals rather than the boys who had labored to care for them.

Tomorrow they would have a hog killing. Everyone would stay home for it would take many hands to kill, scald, and butcher four top hogs. Harry and Mary practically cheered the opportunity. Nadine could only think of the fresh meat they would enjoy and she was happy to face the hard work in order to get that meat.

Jerry had been preparing for this day for weeks. He'd built a wooden trough and lined it with scrap tin. As Jimmy went to put down the animals, Jerry soaked the outer wood and carefully built a fire around the tub. Lou and Roberta carried endless buckets of water to fill the trough and soon the water was near boiling. One after another, each hog was hoisted whole into the scalding water. After a few minutes, Jimmy declared it had been long enough and everyone grabbed the long pole that ran through the tied feet and hoisted the two hundred pounds of pork onto waiting boards to be scraped.

In turn, all four of the big pigs were prepared for the butchering. By the time all of the scraping was finished, Nadine could hardly stand.

"Mother, you need to take a rest," Roberta urged her.

"I can't be resting when you are all working so hard."

"This is too hard on you somehow, just go inside. When you feel better, maybe you can help some more. It's up to the boys to cut out the big hams and shoulders now anyway."

Nadine decided to take her daughter's advice and went in to slowly prepare the family's supper. Lou had already left in the dry sink a pan filled with pigs feet. After a strong cup of coffee and slice of bread, Nadine turned to cleaning the feet and setting them to boil in a big pot. Pigs' feet were never cured with the side meat and hams, so the children considered them a special treat after hog-killing. With fried potatoes and hot cornbread, she would place a feast before her family this night. Surely even Bill would enjoy this meal.

By the time Bill had closed up the store, the short winter day was gone and darkness surrounded the little house. The work was mostly finished on the hogs and everything was secured in the barn lest hungry animals feast on it in the night. Everyone was so tired the supper table was completely silent.

The fat had been cut from the animals and sat in tubs in the kitchen floor. Roberta kept eyeing it through the meal, calculating how long it would take to render lard from all of that. Mother already had her largest pot on the back of the stove slowly cooking down the snow white blubber into the precious staple of the mountaineer's diet. Stored and sold in big metal cans, the lard would bring a healthy price in the store. Roberta was already planning to hide away at least one stand for the family to use.

The smell of the processing lard was strong in the kitchen, but no one complained for they knew tomorrow they would enjoy the cracklin's that were the by-product of this process. Each child thought their mother's 'fatty bread' was as good as molasses cake.

Bill questioned his children about the day's work. Had they wasted any meat? Were they sure they'd cleaned the meat well or was it all going to spoil?

"Most folks killed their hogs in November so we can probably sell all that meat without even having to cure it," he declared.

Jimmy looked at his father, then his mother with an unspoken question. *Surely we won't sell all of that!* He decided he'd have to take care of some of the meat himself. There was a little shack down near the creek and at first light, he removed a ham, a shoulder and a large slab of side meat to that shack. He reminded himself that he'd have to come back later and salt it. This would feed the family many meals.

Bill was in fact able to sell a great deal of the meat fresh. Most of the miners did not keep their own stock and they had been buying cured meat from various peddlers for months. The fresh pork was a welcome change to them. Bill boasted to the family about how much he'd profited on the hogs. He was planning to buy more just as soon as the roads were fit to go find a farmer who had some to sell.

The days began to grow longer and the sun to warm the earth; spring was just around the corner. By early March, Nadine had mustard greens, lettuce, onions, turnips, peas and a few early potatoes planted. The children were looking forward to the end of their school term and spirits that had been dampened by the hard winter were brighter with each new day.

But Bill Lewis was growing restless. He complained about everything. The children made too much noise. Nadine was spending too much time in her garden. The customers were too demanding.

Nadine tried to remind him how well he was doing in the store but he ignored her encouragement. She showed him the children's progress with their studies and how strong each seemed, explaining they had rarely had a winter with so little sickness. Bill found miseries in his own health to complain about.

Then one evening when he and Nadine were alone he announced he would go to East Tennessee on a buying trip for the store. "Maybe the customers will be more satisfied if I bring in new merchandise."

"Can't you have everything brought in on the railroad?" she questioned him.

"Wouldn't be the same. I need to go an' pick out the best stuff. Besides, you have to be on site to get the best deals. You know how I hate to get beat in a deal."

"Have you heard Jimmy talking about getting back to Campground as soon as there's a fit Sunday? I think he will marry this spring."

Bill just grunted, acknowledging that he'd heard her but adding no comment about his son's future.

Nadine sought to entice her husband to stay home with other reasons. "You know, Harry has done really well in school this year, but he doesn't want to go. He is much more likely to keep at his studies if you are here to encourage him."

"He's big enough to know he needs to get his learnin'."

"If Jimmy marries, I think Jerry won't be far behind. Pansy Austin has a sister named Vera, that he's awfully partial to."

"Jerry is only eighteen years old. How can he keep a wife?" Bill was growing increasingly surly with this conversation.

Finally, Nadine offered what she thought was an inarguable reason for Bill to stay home. Softly she said, "Bill, we will have another child by the fall."

He turned his head to his wife and a brief glint of joy sparkled in his eye. It lasted only a moment and then he simply shook his head.

Nadine realized he would go on his trip. She also had long since realized when he went East the trips lasted months. A thousand questions flooded her mind, where would the family stay? Would they try to keep the store open? Would both Jimmy and Jerry leave her so that there was no man left in the house?

Bill turned out the lamp and Nadine closed her eyes in silent prayer, *Lord, I can do nothing about this. I am once again at your mercy.*

Sleep came quickly for Nadine worked hard throughout the day. As she drifted off, she was reminded, *Every good gift and every perfect gift is from above...*

Chapter 11

As the April sun warmed his back, Jerry ran his hand along the lead horses' withers, smoothing the harness' hip strap and setting the breeching. He was proud to be driving the rig into town and he cared little that his errand was to send his father off for an undetermined amount of time. He would return with needed supplies for the store, Jimmy would continue to tend the store for a few more weeks, then Jerry would take over that work when Jimmy left to marry his sweetheart.

The warm, spring weather had allowed Jimmy to make several trips to Campground and he had announced to his family that he would be leaving to marry Pansy in just a few weeks.

Bill was not happy with that announcement. The words father and son shared had been loud and ugly. Bill didn't really trust Jimmy running his store, and he was sure that neither Jerry nor Roberta were smart enough with numbers to keep things running. Finally, he declared, "By-jingo, it'll all be run in the ground by the time I can get back." Still, Bill prepared to make his journey.

Jimmy was unmoved. He had made a plan for his own future and he would go ahead with that plan.

Jerry was pleased to be able to tend the store. He felt certain he could manage and somewhere deep-down, he wanted to prove that to his father.

Bill emerged from the house wearing his long duster. He always wore that coat when he was leaving on a long journey. His boots were polished, his trousers pressed. Jerry took a second look, realizing he was wearing new trousers.

The drive to Monterey seemed much longer than ten miles. Jerry had feared his father would complain about everything from aching joints to the high price of coffee. Surprisingly, Bill Lewis was almost jovial on this drive. That sudden change in his nature put Jerry on guard.

He seems so happy to be leaving us, Jerry thought. He just shook his head and let his father rattle on about first one thing then another.

They could hear the train pulling into the depot as they drove down Monterey's main street.

"Give 'em a little slap there Jerry. The train has to take on water and coal here but I sure don't want to be climbing on as it's pulling out of the station."

Jerry clicked his tongue at the horses urging them in to a slow trot. When he stopped beside the little depot, freight was still being loaded into the boxcars.

Bill's last words to his son were directions for the supplies. He said no farewells.

Bill removed his hat as he walked into the half-full train car. He smiled as he realized there were padded seats on this car. *Trains are gettin' better*, he thought to himself. *Used to have to sit on a hard bench.*

He nodded his head at a couple of men who looked him in the eye. And to one pretty lady, he shot a one-sided smile that caused her to jerk her gaze back to the activity on the rail yard.

He was seated by a window, with his feet propped on the facing seat as the conductor quickly walked the aisle announcing the train's imminent departure. The whistle blew loudly and steam rushed down the sides of the foremost cars as the engine made her first lumbering efforts to pull the cars.

Bill took another look out at the little town. He felt no emotion leaving it. He'd found little joy here this winter, just hard work, a worrisome family and nagging wife.

As the train followed its southeasterly course toward Crossville, he couldn't help but notice the green cast to the forest as springtime crept its way up the mountainside. The train made a brief stop in Crossville, taking on additional passengers and freight. Soon, the big engine chugged out of the station and very quickly began the thousand foot descent to Harriman. The green of the trees seemed to grow deeper with every turn of the iron wheels, and a smile crept over Bill's face. The beauty of the springtime was brightening his dark heart.

The gentle rocking of the train lulled Bill and the sharp whistle announcing their arrival in Harriman snapped him back to reality. He moved with the mass of people quickly exiting the train. He would have to board another which would carry him through Knoxville to his destination in Strawberry Plains.

There was no delay in Harriman. The two competing rail lines quickly off loaded both passengers and freight, everything was re-loaded in the eastbound train and departed quickly. Bill didn't even complain about having to change trains or give up the upholstered seat The Tennessee Central car had offered. He settled himself in the overcrowded dining car where he purchased a sandwich and coffee and took a look around at his fellow passengers. Bill spent some time chatting with other passengers before making his way back to the coach for the rest of the trip. When the conductor announced the Knoxville stop, he passed the sleeping Bill Lewis and woke him only as they neared Strawberry Plains.

The sight of the approaching depot with its twin chimneys and four-sided porch again brought a smile to Bill's face as he stretched his arm and back muscles. He stepped from the train with a lighter heart than he'd felt in many weeks. His hand brushed the wallet in his coat pocket and he was reassured that there was money for his needs as he turned toward the small livery stable.

In the hired buggy, he drove directly to a little building on the edge of town. He knew the place well and the burly man watching the door greeted him by name. Far enough away from the prying eyes of town's folk and railroad employees, a strong drink could be had in this place despite the Prohibition laws. However, no offer was made to Bill for the bartender knew well this man would waste none of his money drinking. Bill had tried to find joy in a bottle many years ago. In fact, after Ann Lewis' death, the bottle was the first place he turned. At the bottom he found a headache and an empty pocketbook but no joy. Then, he continued his quest. Today, he would see if a few hours in a card game could grow the money in his pocket. Surely fortune was the path to real joy.

The game was already underway when he politely filled an open chair. With a neat stack of bills at his fingertips, he picked up the hand of cards. After two hours, his stomach was growling and he had only broken even. He said his goodbyes and climbed back into the buggy.

The squat little house to which he was heading was only minutes from the tavern. He whistled as he pulled into the drive and watched a girl not much beyond toddler years scurry quickly inside. Immediately, a short woman with jet-black hair stepped into the doorway. The keen nose, prominent cheekbones and dark eyes bespoke her Cherokee heritage despite the worn cotton dress and apron she wore.

"Evenin' Mercy. By-jingo that Sulie runs every time she sees me drive in. Can't you make her act more civilized? Have you got supper cooked, I'm starved. Been down at the tavern but you know there's no decent food to be had there. It's highway robbery what they want to charge a man for a bite."

This monologue lasted while he tied the horse and he was now standing toe to toe with the little woman. "Well, woman are ya' gonna let me in my house or not?"

Chapter 12

Mercy watched Bill stroll into the little house as though he had only been gone a few hours. How long had it been this time, she wondered. She had long ago stopped counting the weeks and months when he was away. Tonight she neither asked about his whereabouts, nor did she care where he'd been.

Bill went directly to the pot that was simmering on the wood stove. As he lifted the lid, he looked toward Mercy. "Where'd that Sulie go? And why does she disappear when I ride up?"

Mercy moved quickly inside to take charge of her kitchen. Her tone was sharp as she answered his questions, "She runs because you are a stranger Bill."

"Well that's just ridiculous now, ain't it? Her own daddy can't be a stranger."

Mercy did not respond. She placed bowls on the table and ladled the hearty stew into them. As Bill took the seat at the head of the table, she sliced bread and placed butter and jam before him as well.

Bill was talking about the day's train trip and the news he'd gathered at the tavern. Mercy heard him but scarcely listened to the words. She prepared food for her daughter and placed it on the table at the opposite end from Bill. Tsula would need to eat and since there was no way to know how long Bill would stay this time, Mercy needed to get her daughter used to his presence. Bill was still talking when she walked out of the kitchen into Tsula's small bedroom at the back of the house.

"Tsula," she called gently. Tsula was on the floor, playing with her handmade dolls and looked up at her mother's familiar voice. "Dear, you will have to come eat your supper."

"Is that man still here?"

"Yes, honey he is. He's eating his supper too. Come on now, he won't hurt you."

Tsula obeyed her mother and reached for the outstretched hand. As they returned to the kitchen, it seemed as though the man had never stopped talking.

"Good stew. Deer? Where'd you get it?"

As Mercy seated Tsula and took her own seat, she looked at Bill Lewis wondering if she should even grace his questions with answers. She pondered, *Does he not wonder how we keep from starving to death?*

She chose to answer his questions because she thought it would shame him. "My brothers share their meat with us. We have little way to get food otherwise."

Bill either didn't catch or chose to ignore the barbed comment. "Them boys are still fine hunters. And you've got jam on the table. You do just fine in the kitchen, Mercy."

Despite their proximity to the booming town of Knoxville, Mercy's family clung to many of their ancestors traditions and that was always reflected in their food. However, Mercy loved jam the first time she ate it as a child and whenever she could come by the sugar, she always preserved wild berries in jam.

"The blackberries are plentiful and Tsula and I gather everything we can." She didn't share with him how hard she had to work to get sugar for the jam, nor what a precious treat it was. Mercy Lewis was too proud to let this man know that she slaved all summer growing every vegetable the little plot of land could produce. She refused to admit the shameful way some of her white neighbors spoke to her when she carried baskets full of those vegetables, hoping to sell them for a few pennies to buy the staples she could not grow. Bill seemed not to care what happened to his wife or daughter when he was gone for weeks and months at a time and she would not ask him to care.

With his plate emptied the second time, Bill stretched and patted his stomach, announcing his journey had tired him and he was headed to bed. Neither mother nor daughter responded to him.

Tsula helped her mother clear and wash the dishes without complaint. With the kitchen in good order, the pair quietly padded back to Tsula's little room. Mercy looked around, proud of what she had been able to provide for her daughter. A thick straw tick made a nice bed for her, it lay on a simple bedstead her own father had built. While the brightly colored quilt didn't match the floral curtains, the combination lent a cheery air to the room. Rough shelves on two walls held dolls and puzzles that Tsula's uncles and grandmother had made for her.

Tsula picked up her favorite dolls now, handing them to Mercy, "Tell me a story about these two."

Mercy smiled. It was a game they often played. "Okay, tell me their names and I'll start the story while you put on your nightgown."

Mercy began to weave a story about two Cherokee maidens who went on an adventure down the great river. As the plot progressed, Tsula's head became heavy against her mother's shoulder. Still quietly talking, Mercy covered her daughter then gently slipped into the bed beside her.

Mercy was awake with the sun and stirring the kitchen fire when Bill joined her.

"Where'd you sleep Mercy?" Bill grumbled. "That 'ole straw tick needs your warmth, ya' know."

Mercy continued her work and quietly answered, "No, I didn't know."

In fact, Mercy scarcely knew what Bill wanted from her. It had been ten years since her father brought this strange white man home to their squat, little hut. Bill Lewis strode into that house the same as he came into this one, as though he owned it. Her father looked beat as he introduced them. When he announced that Mercy would go with this man, her mother gasped. Mercy simply questioned, "Doda? Where do I go? Why are you sending me away?"

As the story unfolded, her mother became more and more distraught. Her father had gambled with this man. There was strong drink and he could never handle the drink. In a desperate final hand, he wagered his unwed daughter, hardly thinking what would happen to her until he realized he'd lost the game. Now, he must surrender her to this stranger who said he wasn't interested in a squaw.

With a strength wrought of generations of hardship, Mercy squared her shoulders and sought to comfort her mother. She knew there would be time for her own tears later – she could mourn her lost life for the remainder of her years.

Bill had turned to her father and talked about the girl as though she were nowhere near him. "She is very beautiful. I imagine she will make some man quite happy – might as well be me."

Bill faced the door expecting his new possession to obediently follow him but Mercy did not budge. When the stranger turned to face her she answered before he could question why she had not followed.

"I will not add to my father's shame by refusing. But I know the same Jesus you follow and I know I must not go away if I am not your wife."

Bill hesitated only a moment, then he asked for the local preacher-man as though requesting only a glass of water.

The mission-trained Cherokee sensed the heavy mood when Mercy's father brought him into the house. But apparently he understood the situation and he performed the ceremony without question. Mercy left that night with Bill, having no idea where he'd take her or if she'd ever see her family again.

She was thankful when their journey ended at the little tavern and he opened a door to his rented room. He was kind to her and for that she was thankful. However, he told her nothing of what their life together would be like – not even where they would live.

That first morning, Mercy had thought of the training her mother had given her for this day. *Aluli, here I am a wife but I'm not sure how to start. There is no place to cook, no home to keep.* She found herself mentally reaching out to her mother and it made her terribly homesick. Finally, she told herself, *You don't even know if you will ever see Aluli again so you'd better stop this.*

After a week in the rented room, Bill announced that they could stay there no longer. He took Mercy to a tiny hut he'd rented. Mercy was thrilled with the little place because it was still very close to her family. After a few more weeks, Bill left the little house early one morning saying he was going off on business. Mercy didn't think to ask how long or where he was going. There was little food in the house and she certainly had no money.

Weeks passed and Bill did not return. Mercy soon realized she was expecting his child, but had no way of sharing that joyous news with him. Still more time slowly crept by and Mercy saw that she would be unable to forage for enough food to sustain this new life within her. Swallowing her pride, she went back to her family who she knew would feed her. However, she refused to stay with them, and walked many miles back and forth to the house Bill had left her in.

When the owner of the little hut arrived asking for more rent money, Mercy again turned to her family. They had no money but her brothers quickly built a cabin for her on unclaimed land. By this time, Mercy was less concerned with how Bill would find her.

Bill returned after six months. By that time, Mercy had lost the baby and felt a growing bitterness toward her husband. She was sure the baby would have survived had she had proper food and not been forced to walk in all kinds of weather back and forth to the Cherokee village. When he entered the little house, he offered no apologies or explanations. She told him about the child and he barely responded to her. She boldly questioned him about where he'd been and why it had been so many months. Bill refused to answer; he simply acted as though nothing out of the ordinary had happened.

Chapter 13

Coins jingled in Bill's pocket. He almost always had money when he came home, but Mercy never asked for any of it. Of course he didn't offer her anything either. However, when he headed out for Strawberry Plains, planning to return the rented buggy, he did ask what she might need in the house.

Mercy's pride was not so strong that she would allow her precious Tsula to suffer if there was any opportunity to get the things they really needed.

"We are very low on sugar, and Tsula's dresses are quickly growing too short so I could certainly use some cotton yardage."

Bill was nodding his head. She knew he would not forget any item on a list, although he might just ignore some things she asked for. "I can get a ten pound bag of sugar and you could use the bag. That'd be enough for a dress her size, wouldn't it?"

Mercy smiled and nodded, perfectly willing to reuse the cotton sack. Still, she couldn't help but think of the money she knew he carried. And then there were the clothes that he wore – there were no sugar sacks in his wardrobe. Mercy chose not to mention this. She would take what she could get from this man who gave so little to his family.

Bill had not yet left when Mercy heard her brother calling her as he approached the house. The family always announced themselves well before reaching the door, and both Mercy and Tsula would be excited and rush out and meet them. When only Tsula greeted her uncle, and when he saw the shiny buggy near the front door, he knew without questioning that Bill Lewis had returned.

"Your father has come home?"

Tsula looked up at her uncle, nodding her head. She was completely comfortable with this dark-skinned man, unlike the father who sat at the table with her this morning. In fact, Uncle Adam Hawk was something of a hero to the little girl. He often arrived with a dolly made of cornhusks or a puzzle of wood and string. And he always hugged her and he never left without saying 'good bye'. But this man in her house, this man Aluli called 'Bill', he barely spoke to her and he left without a word.

Uncle Adam was turning into the house, holding Tsula's hand as Bill stepped out.

"Well Adam, howdy there. You're looking fine today – strong as ever aren't you?" Bill greeted his brother-in-law as though they were close friends.

Adam looked directly at the man, conveying his deep dislike only from his piercing eyes. His father had died from a broken heart for this life that he'd sold Mercy into and the Hawk sons held Bill Lewis directly responsible for their father's decline.

Bill continued, seemingly unaware of the penetrating stare. "Had some awfully good venison last night. Not a bit gamey, you sure know how to drop 'em. What did you take that with?"

"We no longer use the long bow Bill," Adam said flatly.

Bill chose to take the words as a joke and laughed jovially. He didn't notice that Adam's stern look was unchanged. "Well, you're as good a shot with a gun as I've ever seen. Now, if you let a deer run after he's hit, there ain't a woman around what can get the gamey taste out. But you drop 'em right in their tracks, don't ya'?"

Adam could only think how ridiculous this conversation was. He had no desire to talk about hunting tactics with this man. He never knew of Bill to hunt when he was home with Mercy, never knew of him to do anything towards providing for and keeping his family. Adam had filled that role, along with his brothers Abraham and Amos, ever since they built the little house for Mercy. Adam considered this his responsibility just as he readily accepted responsibility for providing Tsula with a fatherly influence. It was clear she would get no such guidance from Bill.

Adam stepped into the house, ducking to clear the low doorway.

"O-si-yo my brother," Mercy greeted him from her kitchen, using the traditional Cherokee that peppered their daily language. She'd watched the exchange between Adam and Bill, hearing a few of their words through the open door.

"O-si-yo. When did he arrive?"

Mercy watched as Bill stepped up into the shiny buggy and lightly slapped the horse with the reins. "Last night, just in time for his supper."

"Oh, that's when he ate the deer. He enjoyed it." Adam's voice held a sneer, showing no pride in the compliments Bill had given him. "Is he leaving already?"

"Said he was going into Strawberry Plains to return the buggy. It's rented." Mercy made no effort to defend her husband's actions, nor did she show any faith that he would actually return today. She had long ago given up counting on this man. If he returned today with sugar in a cotton sack, she would be thankful. If not, she would make do with something else.

"I just stopped by to check on you. I am planting today and wanted to share seeds with you." He dropped a small canvas bag on the table. "Do you want me to help you work your garden plot?"

Mercy smiled, she was truly grateful for her brothers. "You have your own work. I will do what I can and when you are finished with your fields, I will welcome your help."

He nodded as he stood, laying a hand on Tsula's hair. As he gently pulled one dark braid he said, "Little Tsula will help you I know. Do you have the hoe I made for you last year?"

Tsula nodded vigorously, setting the braids swinging. "It was too big last year, but this year I am big. I am sure I can help with it."

Adam bent to kiss her scalp, "I know you will do your best. I will be back in a couple of days to see what you have accomplished."

The eldest of the Hawk children stepped out the door and was gone across the field without another sound. Somehow the generations of hunters and trackers remained with him and he could cover long distances remarkably quickly and silently.

Mercy hung the wet towels and took another look at her kitchen. Satisfied that everything was neat and orderly, she turned to her daughter. "Well, Tsula, we mustn't let Uncle Adam's seed waste. Let's get out there in our garden."

The bare patch of ground yielded rich, black soil to Mercy's spade. Again and again she burrowed the steel tool deep into the earth and leveraged the handle down to create the loose tillage her seeds would need to thrive.

She worked through the noon hour. Tsula was accustomed to her mother getting lost in her work so when hunger called her back into the house, she returned with a thick hunk of bread and a slab of cheese she'd found on the kitchen table. Hands that seemed to carry as much dirt as her child-sized hoe did not hinder her lunch. She had worked hard trying to imitate her mother's movements. With her food eaten, she fell asleep watching Mercy continue to turn over shovels-full of soil.

Tsula was back at her mother's side when they heard the familiar, tuneless whistle announcing Bill's return. *So he has come back,* Mercy thought to herself. She looked to the western horizon, judging the time by the quickly setting sun.

"Well, Tsula, we've accomplished much today, don't you think?"

Tsula stood, kneading her back as her mother did and wiping her free hand across her brow. "Hard work Aluli."

Mercy smiled, "Yes, dear. Hard work but it will be worth it when we have vegetables to eat and extra to sell."

Hand in hand they walked the short distance back into their little house where Bill had already made himself comfortable.

"Mercy! Where have you been? It's nearly dark and there's not a thing cooking."

Mercy glared at him momentarily but had no energy for anger. "Tsula and I have turned our garden plot today. We will eat cold meat and bread."

Bill made a face and grumbled under his breath.

Mercy's attention was on Tsula. "Before we do anything, we have to clean up one little ge-hu-ts. You have as much dirt on you as we left in the garden." The two laughed as Mercy heated water and began letting down the child's braids for a good brushing.

Bill largely ignored the family interchange; he busied himself with a newspaper he'd brought home as he waited for Mercy's attention to turn to him.

Chapter 14

The sun was just cresting above the distant mountain as Jimmy entered the store. He smiled as he raised the shades and felt the warmth bathe his face. Jimmy seemed to be smiling a lot these days.

Turning to the stove, he stirred the ashes searching for a glowing coal. This strange season of the year begged a bit of heat in the mornings then, by the afternoon, sun drove him to open every door and window. Finding one of yesterday's embers, he thrust in corn cobs and chips of wood.

There was comfort in this morning routine, and Jimmy had grown to greatly enjoy it. In the weeks since his father left the store in his care, Jimmy had settled into the storekeeper's role. The ledgers assured him that he no longer had anything to prove to Bill Lewis for he had shown a good profit. When the stock ran low, Jimmy wrote to the suppliers and shortly took the team and wagon to receive the goods from the rail so that the shelves had never been bare.

Sure, some of the customers asked about Bill, when he might be returning and wondering where he might be for so many weeks. They were neighbors as well as customers so they were concerned about the squat little man they'd enjoyed doing business with. This was the only time Jimmy struggled with the customers. He wondered how could they be so worried about father? Jimmy reminded himself that these folks in Cliff Springs scarcely knew the Lewis family and wouldn't be aware of Bill's routine absences from his family. So, he answered as vaguely and kindly as he could.

The silence of the empty store was broken as Jerry and Roberta swung the back door open.

"I'm going to re-arrange that pile of fabric this morning. It will surely sell better if the ladies can see what we really have. There're some very pretty pieces on the bottom of the stack." Roberta always knew what she wanted to do when she entered the building and she would argue until Jimmy or Jerry agreed with her – or otherwise she'd just go on doing what she planned while she ignored her brothers.

Jerry was shaking his head, "You really need to get the lamps dusted. Jimmy says only clean things sell." Jimmy had been carefully teaching Jerry everything he knew about merchandising and Jerry was eager to learn and to put his lessons into practice.

"You dust while I arrange this fabric," was Roberta's quick solution, announced as she hurried to that corner of the room.

Jerry was left at the long counter, watching his sister bustle through the tables that were stacked high with all of the necessities of a home and farm.

Jimmy grinned at their argument, thankful that they were serious about the care of the store. He had every intention of standing before the preacher at Campground within the month to marry Pansy Austin but he did not want to carry any guilt that his step-mother and siblings would be in need while he was starting his new life.

As he stepped onto the wide front porch, broom in hand, his mind replayed the conversation he'd had with Nadine just a few days ago.

"Mother, I've decided I can't wait until every little detail is settled here before I marry Pansy. It just ain't right to ask her to wait and wait, is it?"

"No Jimmy, that wouldn't be right. And it's time you start your own llfe." But the deep crease between her eyes didn't look as sure as she sounded.

"What's worrying you Mother?"

She smiled at him, that warm mother's smile that cured all ills and comforted all hurts. "Oh, my dear Jimmy, I've just relied too much on you. We will be fine, and I really meant what I said. You and Pansy deserve to get your life and your family started. The children will miss you terribly though."

"And there's going to be another one, ain't there?"

Nadine blushed scarlet. She had not told the children about the new brother or sister they could expect in the fall and this certainly wasn't a decent topic to discuss with her grown son. She simply nodded her head as she avoided Jimmy's eyes.

Jimmy muttered something under his breath that Nadine was certain was both foul and directed toward his father.

"Jimmy, you must remember that babies are God's gift to man. And I'm so thankful to be able to give your father another one. He seemed pleased when I told him before he left."

"But he left anyway, didn't he?"

"Well, now you know that he had to go buy stock for the store."

Jimmy's voice was rising now, "Stock! I bought stock and never traveled further than Monterey and was home in time for supper."

Nadine wrung her hands unconsciously. *How do I urge these boys to respect their father? Lord, I'm afraid I'm failing my sons.*

Looking Jimmy squarely in the eye she tried to gently explain, "Jimmy, we must trust that your father is doing the very best he can for us. He is a troubled soul, you know, always searching for some elusive joy. One day he'll realize that the joy of The Lord is all around us."

Jimmy just shrugged his shoulders as he turned to leave the room. "Well I just hope you haven't all starved to death before he finds his *joy*."

Nadine watched as the door slammed behind Jimmy. A single tear escaped her eye.

The jingle of horse harness brought Jimmy's mind back to the present. "Mornin' Mr. Taylor. Gonna be a fine one, ain't it?"

"Whoa girls," called the wiry man atop the rough farm wagon as he stood to fully press the wooden brake against the rolling wheel. He nodded at Jimmy as he spoke, "Reckon it will be. Won't make no difference in the dark hole of that mine though. It's the same down there whether it's sunny or rainy."

Jimmy smiled at his neighbor. There was money to be made working in the mines, but it was a hard life, he knew. The miners tended to be a bit sullen, always tempering any happy comment with a bit of pessimism. But they faithfully brought their script to the store and the Philips had never yet failed to pay off for it at special rates Bill had negotiated with them. So, Jimmy would continue to try to please this gloomy lot.

Jimmy let Mr. Taylor go on in the store as he finished his morning sweeping. He was taking pride in the appearance of the store – more pride than he'd been able to muster when his father was home ordering every move. After a few weeks of running the place, Jimmy found he liked the merchant's work and he'd begun to hope to have a store of his own when he and Pansy were married.

Pansy. The thought made him smile. Yet, he rarely thought of her and his new life without also thinking of his siblings and their welfare. He looked across the small yard separating the store from the little house. The chickens were busy pecking at the ground around the back porch. Harry was responsible for feeding and watching after them and he was thrilled with the duty. Although he tried to sound as unconcerned as his older brothers, Jimmy could see that he loved these hens as pets.

Movement near the barn drew his eyes to the fattening hogs there. It was actually too early to be feeding hogs for winter, but Jimmy wondered if they might try to kill one as soon as the first cool day of fall hit. The family was in need of meat and he knew all of the neighborhood would buy fresh meat by then. That would have to be something that Jerry took care of for Jimmy had no intention of staying that long.

Satisfied with the porch's condition, Jimmy returned to his post behind the heavy wooden counter. Jerry had taken care of Mr. Taylor's needs and the two were talking. Jerry had proven to be a gifted carpenter, but he did just fine working in the store too when he was needed.

They'll be just fine, Jimmy told himself. *Today's Friday. I'm going to Campground on Sunday and marry that pretty little Austin girl.* Again he smiled.

Chapter 15

The morning sun warmed Mercy's head as she bent over her green bean plants. As she reached for the weeds she began to notice the first little lilac-colored blooms and they brought a smile to her face. She paused for a moment, thinking of the date – the crop would have been in the ground for just about a month now.

She thought to herself, *Ah, I planted them the day after Bill came in. A month is about as long as he'll stay.*

The thought brought relief to her mind and she looked over to her daughter, always concerned how these visits from her father would affect the girl. Tsula played nearby, wanting desperately to help her Aluli but finding it difficult to focus on the weeds that she was supposed to be pulling. Instead, the crawling red lady bugs fascinated her and the daisies that sprung up at the garden's edge drew her attention.

Mercy smiled at her, thankful that she could enjoy her little-girl life. At least these days with Bill at home were safe for both mother and daughter; at least Bill didn't drink and come home in the violent tempers she knew some of the Cherokee men did. Stretching her back, Mercy looked up at the quickly warming sun and knew there were many blessings she must count.

It's been a long time since I thanked God for these blessings. But instead of praying as her own Aluli had taught her, she simply lowered her head. The missionaries had taught her from an early age that she must pray every day and for a long time she had done so. Even now, the sun on her face, the crop that grew green in the little plot of ground, and certainly her daughter's giggles assured her that God had not abandoned her. She often asked herself why she no longer talked to him, but she found no easy answer.

She'd left the squat little house without preparing a hot breakfast this morning. In fact, Bill had still been sleeping when she fed Tsula yesterday's bread and a chunk of cheese. When she heard the click of the back door, she knew his words before he spoke them.

"Mercy, have you let me sleep through breakfast and you didn't save me any. Why, there's not even hot coffee made."

"No Bill," she called to him. "We ate bread and cheese only. I wanted to get to work on these weeds as early as possible."

Bill was stepping across the neat rows, one hand on his back. Mercy felt a moment's compassion for she knew arthritis plagued his back and legs; she was certain he was suffering this morning. She smiled, thankful that she was still able to have at least a moment's compassion for this man she must call 'Uyehi' despite his unwillingness to truly live as a husband. There was yet another blessing she should really be thankful for, a heart not completely hardened by bitterness.

Bill caught sight of the smile and believed it was for him. This lovely little woman had not brought him the joy he'd hoped for when he said vows before her parents and the mission's preacher-man. But no man would be unmoved by a smile from such a woman. He straightened a bit more despite the pain in his back. He'd awoken cursing the straw tick that covered both the beds in the little house and swearing he'd sleep on a soft, hotel bed tonight.

Now, as he watched Mercy return to her work, her slender figure silhouetted by the bright morning sun, he wondered if perhaps he should spend another week here. Mercy had shone no affection for him for the past month and that was one of the biggest reasons he thought he should head into Knoxville this day. After all, there were friends there that might be a bit more welcoming to him.

He reached Mercy's side and laid a hand on her shoulder, expecting her to respond warmly. Instead she simply ignored him continuing her steady work ridding plants of the unwanted weeds.

"Well I guess I need to get into Knoxville today," Bill announced after a moment. "That's near twenty miles, gonna need something hot in my stomach for that trip."

Mercy paused only a split second. Biting back sharp words, she straightened and attempted to brush away the dirt from both hands and apron. "Come Tsula, let's go inside for a while."

Normally, Tsula would have begged permission to stay in the garden with the bugs and flowers and all of the imaginary adventure she was having. But she had not missed her Doda's entrance and she almost always chose to just be quiet when he was around. She took one last look at the busy caterpillar she'd been watching and followed her mother inside.

The late breakfast was quickly cooked and served with minimal conversation. Bill appreciated the food Mercy could produce seemingly from nowhere. Hot biscuits that seemed to float from the plate, deer that had been last night's supper was finely chopped and cooked into a thick gravy. And there were eggs. Bill did like eggs.

"Umm-um. What a meal you can put before your man, Mercy. It does make a fellow feel appreciated. Almost hate to leave this good cookin'. 'Course I'll have to stay in the hotel tonight and they sure can't make gravy like you in no hotel."

"Glad you like it Bill," was her only response as she turned to encourage Tsula to eat.

Bill continued to talk about the food and his journey. Mercy gathered that he was buying goods for some business, although she could not imagine who would send him to buy for them, nor why they would allow him to waste so many weeks. She wondered what he'd been doing these past weeks. Each day he walked into Strawberry Plains and spent most of the day there. Once he'd come home with a saddle horse, but he'd only ridden it a few days before he walked home in a foul mood and Mercy reasoned that he had lost the beast as easily as it had been won.

Today Bill left Mercy's house on foot. He wore the long duster coat and he left nothing behind him. As she heard the door click shut, she looked around her home. The cupboards were a little better stocked than when he'd arrived for every time he mentioned to her he was going into town, she'd asked for another staple item. Tsula had her new dress and there were additional sugar and flour sacks that she would be able to sew into needed clothing in the coming weeks.

Bill Lewis never looked back; his mind was already turned to the business and the company he could find in Knoxville. He looked down the dusty road and thought only of making it to the river. Surely there would be a ride from the ferry. His pockets were lighter than he wanted, having had bad luck at the card tables in recent days.

Should'a headed out while I had a saddle horse, he thought and he grumbled beneath his breath. The closer he drew to the river's edge, the more traffic he could see coming from all directions. The ferry had already taken one trip to the west side of the big bend in the Holston River so there would be a short wait. Bill looked around at the other travelers, seeking any hint of interest among them.

By the time the ferry was tied to the pilings on the bank and a couple of wagons rolled off, Bill had struck up a conversation with a farmer carrying a load of rough-hewn rails and travelling alone. There was plenty of room on the wagon seat behind a stout pair of mules and Bill was certain he would be offered a ride. Just to be sure, Bill took hold of one bridle and helped the man coax the mules onto the swaying ferry. He spoke gently to the animals and received hearty thanks once they were tied on the ferry's waiting rail.

As the little flat bottomed transport made its way slowly across the broad river, Bill's eyes were drawn down with the quick moving current. He squinted as though his very will could allow him to see what thrills could be found down river. He knew Chattanooga lay down river and he kept meaning to venture that way, but the railroad was the better way to travel there. His eyebrows rose unconsciously as he wondered if perhaps he should head south instead of going back up the mountain with wares for the Cliff Spring store. He grunted aloud as he pondered what Nadine's boys would have done with the store in the past few weeks.

"What's that buddy?" The old man asked.

Bill hadn't realized how long he'd been silent, nor that his questioning grunt had been audible. "Ah, nothin'. Just wonderin' what my good-for-nothin' boys have done with my store. I been gone buyin' supplies, ya' know."

"Ya got ya' a store?"

"Yeah, little one - serves mostly miners and loggers."

"And ya' got boys big enough and bright enough to run it whilst you're gone?" The old man was looking a little more closely at his newfound friend.

"Well I don't know if they're bright enough. Could be Jimmy, that's my oldest, could be he's run it all in the ground while I've been gone. Prob'y I'll try to sell it when I get back."

"It's not doin' good business?"

"Oh no," Bill assured him, "business has been real good all winter long."

"People not payin' on their 'counts?"

Bill shook his head, "The folks are honest on the mountain. Won't generally try to cut out on a debt."

"Well I don't know why you'd sell it. Sounds to me like you got yourself a fine setup. Good boys that are keepin' store while you're away, a woman waitin' for ya' and a lil' business to keep the wolf from the door. God has smiled on you, ain't he? What'cha gonna' do if ya' sell out?"

Bill shrugged his shoulders. It was the only answer he could offer.

He gladly accepted the expected ride and with a last look down river, he turned to face the city. There'd be good times here for a few days. Maybe he'd regain some of his recent losses then he'd go on up the mountain and rid himself of this burdensome store.

The old man let Bill off on the corner of Jackson Avenue and Gay Street. The sun had already started its decent toward the western horizon and his stomach reminded Bill he hadn't eaten since the fine breakfast Mercy had put before him.

Bill cast a glance toward the warehouses on Jackson; the street fairly buzzed with whirring engines and beeping horns along with the clomping hooves of draft horses and angry voices as the crowd all seemed to be in each other's way. It took him only a moment to decide to go directly to the traditional Irish pub where he knew the food was plentiful and a clean bed could be had upstairs. He cared little for the noise the nearby train tracks would make through the night; the clamor downstairs would drown out most of that.

The Ryans came to East Tennessee in the middle of the last century, certain their pot of gold lay in lands abandoned by the native peoples. However, they found their niche in the New World to be a piece of the old country which they recreated in Ryan's Tavern. Nearly a century later, the steady flow of whiskey had been severely restricted by the Prohibition movement, but honest card games and hearty food kept customers coming and the regulars would find a little something extra in their mugs. "Pap", the current proprietor, had no intention of changing the setup now and when the familiar face of Bill Lewis appeared before his bar he welcomed him as though he were an Irish brother and summoned a girl to bring him food.

Steam spiraled from the bowl of stew on a plate garnished with thick slices of earthy, brown bread and plenty of sweet cream butter. It was much like the food either Nadine or Mercy would place before him, yet Bill failed to realize the irony as he smiled up at the slightly plump waitress and resisted the urge to slap her behind. Instead, he dug into his meal and began to study the game underway at a corner table.

With his stomach satisfied, he placed a few coins on the table and fingered the bills he had left to buy supplies. Mentally measuring how much he was willing to gamble today, he turned toward the poker game. By nightfall, his stack of bills was substantially thicker and he ended his evening in the company of a brightly painted woman with a thick Irish accent. He didn't bother to ask about her accent or her history and he knew that she was only interested in relieving him of some of those bills. He cared little, hoping that her company would further elate the mood so boosted by his winnings.

Three days later, his winning streak began to wane and the Irish brogue to wear at his nerves. He said a friendly farewell to the Pub's owner and turned down Jackson Avenue to see what would interest him to carry back to the store.

Each purchase he ordered delivered to The Southern Railway Terminal and when he arrived to load his freight, he was very satisfied to see how much of the car he'd been able to fill. With ticket in hand for Monterey, he settled himself into the terminal's restaurant to await his train call. With a newspaper and hot coffee, he stretched his legs out to enjoy the wait. He couldn't help but feel he'd made a successful journey and the pride in his accomplishment put a smile on his face.

Chapter 16

Bill stepped off the train at the familiar Monterey depot, his well-polished boots crunching cinders that poured from the big coal burning engine as they rolled into town. He looked around, checking whether he was acquainted with any of the other disembarking passengers and noting the amount of freight being off-loaded. No civic pride swelled within him as he scanned the booming business of the little town; he looked only for opportunities to grow his own fortune.

Pulling a freight manifest from his duster pocket, he walked into the freight master's office to arrange storage of the goods he'd brought from Knoxville.

"Afternoon Alvin," he greeted the familiar face.

With a quick nod, the agent returned the greeting, "Afernoon, Bill."

Waiving his paperwork, Bill continued, "Got a boxcar half-filled with supplies. Can you store them for a day or two. I'll have to get a team and come get 'em."

"Sure thing Bill. You know the rates. Just bring that manifest back when you have your wagon."

Bill strode from the office and crossed a short alleyway to the Imperial Hotel which was known up and down the Tennessee Central rail line for the fine food served there. He intended to have a good meal before making his way back to Cliff Springs.

There's no tellin' whether that woman will have a meal on the table tonight, he thought as his mind turned toward Nadine and his children. As he took his seat he wondered if he should just stay in town rather than making the long walk and maybe not getting home till after dark. But the shrinking roll of bills dissuaded him from overnighting and after a hot meal he headed west.

At the outskirts of town, he heard the jingle of harness approaching behind him and automatically turned to look. The friendly farmer drew up his team and offered a ride.

"I'm headed to Muddy Pond. You kin' ride if you're goin' that way."

Bill was climbing into the tall buckboard before he even answered the man. "Glad to have a ride. I'm only goin' to Cliff Springs."

"Why, it's the store-man, Bill Lewis, ain't it?"

"Yeah, I'm Bill Lewis," he stuck a hand out to his newfound friend.

"Calvin Miller. Ain't seen you 'round in a while. You're boys been runnin' the store ain't they?"

Bill saw an opportunity to learn how badly his sons had failed with the store in their father's absence. "Yep, been on a buyin' trip in East Tennessee. Wonder if the store will even be intact when I get there."

Calvin spit tobacco juice over his left arm before shaking his head at the passenger, "They're good boys, fer as I kin' tell. I's in there just last week and that Jerry took good care of me."

"Jerry? Should've been Jimmy in the store. Jerry's got no head for business at all. Don't know what will ever become of that one."

The two men continued to chat as the team plodded along the muddy road. However, Bill saw no credit in anything this neighbor said. If he couldn't see what good-for-nothings Nadine's boys were then his opinion wouldn't count for much.

As they pulled abreast of the storefront, the sun hung low on the horizon. Bill was sure it would be dark before Calvin could reach Muddy Pond. He chose to stop in the store rather than the house so he could see how badly things had failed in his absence.

As he entered the store, Jerry was as surprised to see his father as Bill was to see his second son.

In unison they asked, "What are you doin' here?"

"It's my store," Bill spat. "I've got better reason than you to be here."

"Well, for the last month, I've been helpin' run it while you've been gone."

Jerry could see the rage creeping up his father's neck, "You? I should have known Jimmy would cut out the minute my back was turned. Should have known I couldn't trust him."

With a final glance around the store, Bill strode out continuing to mutter about the shortcomings of his eldest son. He wasn't finished fussing when he entered the front door of the little house.

Hearing the noise, Nadine peeked around the kitchen door. "Bill! When did you get home?"

He watched his slender, smiling wife move quickly toward him. "Stopped in the store first. Knew that Jimmy would run off the minute I left him in charge. I guess he took the till with him too?"

"What? Jimmy didn't run from anything. I don't understand."

"By-Jingo, I don't know what's to understand. Jimmy ain't in the store, Jerry is. I guess I'm proud that Jerry would stay and try to muddle through but he's got no head for it. I just want to know how much did Jimmy take me for?"

"Bill, I think you are confused. Jimmy has been working very hard in the store and it's done well while you've been away. He left last weekend to marry Pansy Austin in Campground."

Jerry stepped in the door in time to hear his mother's defense of her step-son. He waited for an opportunity to support her.

"The store is filthy, and the books will tell me tomorrow what Jerry's stole. And I'll go to the constable, you can bet I will. Son or not he'll not rob me and get away with it."

Jerry stepped up to try to reassure him. "Father, nothing's been taken. What the books will show you is that business is thriving and the accounts are current. Why, Jimmy actually re-stocked the staples from the profits."

Nadine refused to argue with her husband. The brief defense she offered for Jimmy was as much conflict as she dared. She returned to her kitchen and the supper preparations. At least the meal should please Bill – there were spring greens and a stewed chicken which Lou reported had gotten caught in the fence and had to be killed. She even had dried beans still left from last summer's preserving work. And she had hot cornbread already in the oven. Surely Bill would be satisfied with a feast like this.

Nadine could hear the conversation continuing in the front room. She was surprised that Bill was berating Jerry for the filthy nature of the store; Roberta had been faithfully cleaning there everyday and Nadine knew her daughter would do a good job cleaning. However, she heard her husband saying that Roberta had no business being in the store – 'there's no place for women in business'.

The sound that came from the steep staircase was so small Nadine almost didn't look, but when her eyes darted to that corner and saw Roberta sitting there, she knew that her daughter had heard everything Bill was saying. She dared not go to her to comfort her lest she draw Bill's attention and his verbal attack might spread to her. Roberta's feelings would be terribly hurt for Nadine knew she had greatly enjoyed the work in the store.

She saw a weak smile from Roberta as they both overheard Jerry asserting that 'customers are always asking for Roberta; they really enjoy her'.

Bill just walked away from Jerry's explanations, throwing over his shoulder as he passed through the door, "That girl's not smart enough to work with money."

Nadine's heart broke along with her daughter's. Jerry took a seat at the end of the table and she saw the hurt on his face too.

"Why do I ever expect it to be different?" Jerry asked.

Chapter 17

Bill spent the next two days immersed in the store's records. Try though he may, he could find no dishonesty on Jimmy's part; in fact, the business was even more profitable during his absence than before. All of this good news served to make Bill ever grouchier. He moved about both house and store mumbling to himself; he hardly spoke to any member of his family and wasn't especially kind to his customers.

At breakfast on the third day, he announced that he would take the team into Monterey to retrieve the supplies he'd brought from Knoxville.

Always eager for a trip to town, Jerry quickly volunteered to go for him.

"No, you will tend the store today," Bill declared without further explanation. He picked up his hat, patted his pocket for the necessary paperwork and walked out the back door.

Jerry looked across the table to Roberta, "Well I guess the mess we made in the store wasn't bad enough to let us go into town in his place, was it?"

The siblings shared a quick smile before Nadine's chastening look reminded them that she expected them to respect their father no matter how badly he treated them.

Later in the morning, Roberta joined Jerry in the store and continued her work clearing shelves in the tiny store-room and cleaning space in the store in preparation for the supplies their father would bring home. When the sun began to set and they locked up the business, he had still not returned.

Only Nadine anxiously watched the door during supper and during the time spent cleaning-up afterward. She waited until her eyes refused to remain open and still Bill had not returned. Finally, Nadine slept, knowing that her husband would return in his own good time.

It was two more days before the iron wheels rattled down the rutted lane sending trace chains jingling and harness leather squeaking with every step the horses made.

Jerry was carrying colorfully printed bags of flour out to a waiting rig when he saw his father returning. He was surprised that the wagon was only half full. He couldn't help but wonder, *How did it take him over a month to buy that many supplies?*

Without comment, Jerry walked through the store, out the back door and began off-loading the goods. Bill neither explained nor excused his two day absence. He left the load with his son and headed to the house. Before he entered, he saw Nadine in back with an egg basket on her arm and he walked around to join her.

"Oh Bill, you're home again," she greeted him.

"Yeah." Without allowing a chance for any questions, he announced to her, "I'm going to go to Clarkrange tomorrow and see a man about a farm. I've sold the store. We'll have to be out in a week. Already sold most of the supplies in Monterey."

Nadine was speechless; her hand froze in mid-air, still holding the egg she'd just taken from its nest beneath a wooden box. "What?" was all she could utter.

Bill had already turned toward the house.

"Why? We are doing so well here." Her questions fell on his back and were left unanswered.

As she followed him into the house, Nadine continued to hope for either an explanation, or better still an opportunity to change her husband's mind. However, he explained only his planned trip to Clarkrange.

"Saw a man named Peters in town. He knew of a good farm on The Emery Turnpike that's for sale. Think I'll go make that trade and we'll move there. Seems like it'd feel good to be farmin' again. You know that's what I was doing when I lived under the mountain. 'Cept, I was running the farm for another man, it wasn't my own. Hog farm, ya' know."

Bill rambled with little concern whether Nadine was listening. He poured a cup of coffee from the pot he found on the back of the stove and stepped to the kitchen window sipping it slowly. "I'll get rid of those chickens; nasty things I'd never try to move them. And it's too warm now for hog-killin' so I'll try to sell the ones we have now – too much trouble to run them across the creek when we move."

Nadine wanted to beg him. She wanted to tell him how much little Harry enjoyed the chickens. She wanted to explain how Lou and Mary had worked with the hogs, coaxing them to eat more and more so they would be perfectly fat come cold weather. She longed to tell him that Winnie had made friends with one of the miner's daughters and would be heartbroken to leave her. But more than anything, she wished she could remind him that she was carrying another precious child of his and perhaps it would be best if she didn't pack and move a house just right now.

Somehow, Nadine Lewis knew that none of this would change her husband's mind. As she watched him silently contemplating owning a farm, she thought she saw a glimmer of peace in his eyes. Certainly, he'd always talked about his early days working on the hog farms. That was when he was married to Naomi and Jimmy's mother. She knew those were the happiest days of his life. Nadine would sacrifice any amount of personal comfort or security to give him back that happiness.

She thought surely the children would also be willing to give everything up to return that joy to their father – for maybe that would also give them the father they all longed to have. Nadine realized her children had never really known a father's love.

She couldn't help but smile at the memory of her own father. He was never as successful as Bill, but oh how he loved his family. And he realized that Bill wasn't fully devoted to his precious daughter – but he realized it too late. She remembered the day he'd visited her shortly after Roberta was born. With little Jerry toddling around, he looked at his daughter and grandchildren and begged Nadine to come home with him. "I know Bill will provide for you, that man seems to have a Midas' touch. So your life would be harder but I don't believe you will ever know love here."

Rarely did Nadine scoff but that memory brought her close to it. She looked at the cracked pewter on her table and her children's bare feet and wondered what her father would say about Bill's Midas' touch if he were here now. However, as she looked into the eyes of each son, she realized he'd been right on one point, there was little love in this family.

During the supper hour, Bill handed out duties to each dumb-struck child which would facilitate a quick move. This was not the first time, but his family seemed to never grow used to Bill's sudden changes. Harry simply stared down at the table as he was told he would have to kill every chicken to sell in the store over the next few days. Lou seethed with anger that his and Mary's work with the hogs would be wasted when they were sold so early in the season. Poor Winnie was simply heartbroken to leave her new friends, but she dared not cry. Roberta and Jerry could only shake their heads for they were the most aware of the profit the family left in walking away from the little store.

Each child knew from hard experience that argument would bring no change to their father's made-up mind.

He left again, this time riding one of the horses. Rarely did he leave with his family aware of his plans. As Jerry watched him disappear over the hill he almost hoped this would be another trip that lasted weeks or months. But until he returned, each member of the family would try to do as their father directed – Nadine would insist upon it.

Chapter 18

Though it was scarcely eight o'clock, the summer sun beat down on the Lewis family as Bill turned the loaded wagon onto the dirt road. Nadine couldn't help but look longingly back at her garden, the well-mended corral fence, the chicken coop – all the signs that her family had begun to put down roots in this place. She dropped her head to catch the lone tear that threatened to escape.

Trailing behind, the children were walking to relieve some of the burden from the team. They faced only a six mile walk – a distance any of them would have run under happier circumstances, but no one wanted to leave Cliff Springs.

Jerry smiled and nudged Roberta, "Look at us! We looked about the same when we came to Cliff Springs – din' none of us want to leave Campground."

Roberta wasn't quite as melancholy as her siblings. The emotion she most strongly felt was anger. In fact, she could feel the beginnings of a real bitterness toward her father. "It's not so much leaving the place that bothers me, it's just that we can't ever get ahead. Now we're headed to God only knows what kind of house. You and Lou will have to spend the next month patching to keep out rain and varmints."

Jerry just nodded as he kept up the steady pace behind the wagon.

"Jerry, I'm not going to keep letting him drag me from pillar to post. I'm not willing to work into my adult years to line that man's pockets. I know he's got money and yet we had to sneak to get a single pair of shoes for each of us. Just as quick as I can, I'm going to the store in Clarkrange and see if there's work I can get. I know there are folks that hire girls to help out around the place."

Jerry let out a low whistle for he knew how well that suggestion would go over – even with their mother. She did not want any of her children leaving until they must.

As the team started down the steep hill to ford Hurricane Creek, Bill stood on the brake and cursed his wife's insistence that they load the heavy iron stove. Nadine had dismounted from the wooden seat to walk with the children. Still she heard Bill's complaints but ignored them as she allowed her eyes to caress the blued iron. *I've never owned my own stove in all of my married life. And most of that time I've fed this family from the open flame of a fireplace. I will not feel guilty for this one luxury when we had it sitting in the store that would have just gone to the new owner.*

Of course, Bill had mentioned how much it was costing him, for the more inventory he could show, the higher price paid in turning over the business. None of the family knew quite how much Bill received for the sale, but they were certain he'd turned a profit in addition to the profits they'd seen over the past two years.

The sun stood directly over their heads as they rolled through Campground. Everyone longed to stop in at Naomi's little house below the church, but Bill would not hear of it. Nadine even mentioned trying to find out where Jimmy and Pansy were living but he wasn't interested in that either. They would even wait to eat the cold meat and bread that was packed for lunch until they reached their new home.

Stomachs were rumbling and Harry had given in to ride on the seat beside his mother by the time Bill pointed out the boundary of the property. Nadine strained to see the house, but the big oak trees hid all but the faintest outline. Burned timbers showed the remains of a barn lost no doubt to lightning and a small pond was still covered in green algae nearby.

"Whoa there girls," Bill called to his team, stopping them in the middle of the road. "Just look at this land. Level, with water and half cleared already. Pro'bly too late to get corn in the ground this year, but we can put by enough hay to see the team through the winter. I'll see 'bout getting some sows and maybe I can buy enough corn to get them fattened."

He turned around in the seat to call, "Jerry, you come up here."

Jerry obediently trotted up to the front of the wagon.

"See that barn, we'll have to get a new one up right away. That's what you're good at so I'll leave you to it."

Jerry's heart brightened at the praise his father offered and he looked at the project with new eyes. Yes, he was good at building and with a very little bit of help he'd have the new barn standing in no time. Somewhere deep in his heart he couldn't help hoping that his father would be proud of him for that.

Almost as soon as Bill gave the team the 'Gid-up' command, Nadine began to make out the shape of the house. She studied it, not taking her eyes off it until the wagon drew to a stop in front.

Outside, was a non-descript, single story house with a narrow porch on the front. As Nadine led her family inside, two small rooms presented themselves at the front of the house. Built of rough-sawn boards, this was clearly the newest part. Walking through a wide doorway she found herself in a long, log structure. The open chimney and few cupboards suggested this was the kitchen. She turned a complete circle before she convinced herself there was no fireplace.

"Well, it's a good thing we brought the stove. This is the first house we've ever lived in that had no fireplace at all."

Jerry was at her side, bouncing on the balls of his feet to test the strength of the floor. "Seems sturdy enough." He turned his eyes upward searching for beams of sunlight foretelling leak points. The dark ceiling gave up no secrets of what rains would bring the family. "Guess we'll just have to see how she weathers the first big storm."

With an almost unperceivable shrug of her shoulders, Nadine turned to the work at hand. "Let's get the pictures."

Jerry knew she had decided to make this place her home for the beautifully framed portraits of Bill's parents and his first wife were the first things that were unpacked each time the family moved. Nadine stepped back into the front room and chose spots to hang each one.

Nadine stood before the pictures; with a smile and nod of her head she turned and began directing her family in the unloading of their meager possessions.

With only three rooms to work with, the adult's bed would be placed in the living room, the girls would take the other front room and Jerry, Lou and Harry would have a bed in the kitchen.

It took all the boys working together to haul the iron stove into the log kitchen. Even Bill had to assist. By supper time, they had it connected to the flu and a small fire was burning. Nadine set a simple meal before her exhausted family and they ate in near-silence as they each adjusted to this latest upheaval in their lives.

Chapter 19

"I don't know when's the best time to move to a new farm, but I'm pretty sure June ain't it." Jerry's complaints were offered to anyone within earshot as he fought back thick weeds. Fences in sad disrepair had allowed neighborhood livestock, accustomed to roaming the wooded hillsides, access to the fields. But these fields had seen neither plow nor sickle for many seasons and now the briars and seedling trees threatened to take back the cleared farmland. Broken and scattered rails indicated a garden-spot had once been protected near the house but hungry hogs and cows had long since pushed their way into that plot as well.

"Ain't no use fussin' 'bout it. Father does what he wants whenever the notion strikes. Don't matter whether it's the right time or not. I'm just glad we didn't have to move into the drafty house in the middle of winter." Roberta didn't have to look up as she swung the long scythe from right to left trying desperately to avoid her boots.

Jerry couldn't agree more with the bright spot his sister had found in the whole situation. "Yeah, this winter would have been especially bad. With Mother having a baby and she's not had one for nine years now, she may be sickly, huh?"

Roberta smiled at him. "Now what do you think you know 'bout having babies?"

"Well, I know that we lost that old mare when she couldn't birth her colt. And after all, Jimmy and Naomi's mother died after having Jimmy." The very thought of losing their beloved mother brought Jerry to an abrupt halt.

"Now Jerry, don't you go borrowin' trouble. She brung every one of us into the world without a hitch. Why wouldn't you think she could do it again?"

"Well, she was a lot younger then."

The rhythm of Roberta's tool never slowed and now her head shook in time with it. "She's not even forty, you know."

Jerry looked across the field and saw Lou and their father in the distance. "Well, the old man is back and it looks like they are driving some kind of animals. Wonder what he's bought?"

Roberta took the opportunity to straighten her back while her eyes sought the horizon for her brother and father. "I'm sure it's pigs. That's all he's been able to talk about, how wonderful it was when he ran the hog farms under the mountain. Can't see how it could be so great since they just stink and waller and make a mess."

Jerry couldn't help but smile – girls! "Well you don't think about that when you're eatin' bacon. Anyway, we were makin' good money on the hogs in Cliff Springs."

"And I'm sure he'll make money on these. That man seems to be able to turn a penny into a dollar anytime he wants to. It's just a shame he never even gives pennies to his family."

Lou was within hollering distance in a matter of minutes. Slightly out of breath, he had directions for Jerry. "We need to get the team. Father has traded for a plow and we gotta' go get it. He wants us plowing tomorrow."

"Plowing?" Jerry fairly spit the word out. "What's he want to plow?"

Lou had expected the questions, "Says we got to plant corn to feed these hogs this winter."

"Corn won't never make this time of year. It's too late."

Lou only shrugged and hurried on to the makeshift corral they had built to hold the horses until the barn was raised. He knew that Jerry was following him because he heard his brother's complaints with every step.

When the pair finally reached the corral and began hitching the horses, Jerry shared his thoughts. "I am pretty sick of that old man tugging us first one direction and then the other. I'll not be doing his bidding till I'm twenty like Jimmy did. We're close enough now that I can court Pansy's sister, Vera. And I'm going to get out of here and start my own life."

Lou only nodded. He knew that he would have little chance of getting out of the house for several more years and while he certainly wouldn't ask Jerry to remain on his account, he knew that losing Jerry so quickly after Jimmy leaving home would only make things more difficult for Harry and himself. Lou simply shrugged off the unknown future and turned to the work at hand.

They were just hooking up the freshly harnessed horses to the wagon when Roberta breathlessly flew past them. "Don't leave without me," she called in passing. It took her only moments to return in a clean dress and tying her best straw hat on her head.

"Which way are you going?" The question seemed to be an after-thought. She had assumed they would be going toward Clarkrange. "I want to go to Peters' store."

Lou nodded as he climbed onto the wooden seat, "We're going that direction."

Jerry watched as Roberta scrubbed at the grass stains on her hands with a wet rag she'd brought along. "Why are you working so hard on your hands?"

"I'm going to find work that ain't in them fields or barns. They won't want me workin' in their fine homes if I've got nasty hands, now will they?"

Lou and Jerry shared a questioning look, "Just what fine homes are you talkin' about?"

"Well, anybody that can afford to pay help."

Lou shrugged; Jerry nodded. No more questions were necessary.

Peters' store sat at the intersection of the Emery Turnpike and the Kentucky Stock Road. As the wagon made the turn, Roberta hopped from the back. In two long leaps she was on the store's wooden porch. A quick glance through the tall windows revealed a young woman behind the counter. Taking a deep breath, Roberta walked through the open doors wearing a bright smile.

It was a very short time later that Jerry and Lou started back toward home with the plow loaded. They found Roberta already halfway back, her step seemingly lit with fire.

Jerry called down to her from his seat on the wagon, "The way you're walkin' you can probably beat us home, but we'll give you a ride if you want one."

"Well I'm not going to walk when I can ride. Anyway, I can hardly wait to tell you what I've learned. The girl keeping the store today was Sarah Peters. And she knew of a family nearly in Grimsley that needs some help. She had their address and I've already posted a letter to them."

Both boys had heard Roberta's plans to find work away from home. Still, they were shocked that she had actually gone through with it.

The letter was answered before the week ended and the following week Roberta was ready to leave her family and move to the Bledsoe's. She hinted to her father for a ride to their house but he flatly refused and forbid her brothers to use his team to take her.

She packed everything she owned, or at least everything that was worth taking with her, into a small canvas bag which Nadine stitched just for this purpose. Hugging her mother and each of her siblings, Roberta set out to walk the ten miles to Grimsley.

Her final words were to Winnie, "I'll find something for you as soon as I can."

Nadine waved to her oldest daughter holding back the sobs that threatened to steal her breath. It hadn't been this hard to say good-bye to either Naomi or Jimmy and now she wondered if she really did feel differently about her stepchildren. *No,* she reasoned, *they left for homes of their own. This is hard because Roberta is going out to work for strangers.*

Turning away from the window, she saw the rest of her family and knew she had to be strong and care for them. *Lord, I give Roberta into Your care.*

Bill had no time to bid his daughter farewell. He had chores to assign to Jerry and Lou and Jerry was argumentative about them.

"Don't you think I need to be working on making that house livable? I know it's the middle of summer but if we don't get it sealed up 'fore winter then we'll all freeze. And there'll be a new baby in there this winter; you want him to die of a chill before he even starts to live?"

Bill answered simply, "There's no profit in working on that house."

"Profit?" Jerry was practically shouting now and he lowered his voice only to save the grief he knew his mother would feel if she heard them. "I want you to just tell me why you are always so all fired worried about turning a profit. We were making a good profit in that store and you up and sold it for heaven only know what reasons. And what did it even matter that there was money to be made? You weren't spending one dime on your family. Why, we only have clothes on our backs right now 'cause Roberta just went and took what we needed."

Bill turned red at the revelation that he'd lost merchandise to Roberta. "What? She stole from me? By-jingo, I'll catch her and tan her like she's never known."

Jerry was immediately sorry that he'd let that slip and he desperately wanted to turn the topic back to Bill. With his voice rising he said, "Forget about Roberta. It's you we're talking about. Go on and tell me what is *profit* really for?"

Bill just squinted at him as though he were trying to see through the boy. "Seems like wealth would bring joy, don't it?"

Again Jerry's voice rose, "Joy? You wouldn't know joy if it bit you on the nose."

After a moment's pause, Jerry looked at his father again and seemed to see him in a new light. "What profit is there if your whole family is lost?"

Jerry could no longer stand to look at his father and he stomped off to do the chores he'd been given before he loosed the tirade. He thought he'd feel better after getting it off his chest but it was not better; he still felt angry and bitter and some other feeling that he couldn't quite identify.

As he walked away he told himself, *Roberta had the right idea. I've just got'ta get out of here as quick as I can.*

Chapter 20

The whole family worked hard through the summer months. The boys planted corn when they knew it would never fully mature. Nadine planted the few seeds she had left and tried not to think about the garden they'd left behind in Cliff Springs. However, she couldn't help but remember the relative ease the family enjoyed the previous winter when they not only had the income from the store, but also enjoyed the bountiful produce from their garden. This year there would be little to come from a garden planted when the sun was already so hot it scorched every little leaf that peaked through the hard soil. Still she tried.

She was growing heavier with child and finding her energy waning. By late August there were a few beans to pick but Nadine had to leave it to Winnie and Mary to pick them. She sat under the shade of a big maple tree and slowly strung the beans together for drying.

As she threaded bits of course string onto her needle, her mind ran the gamut of time recounting the years of her married life and the milestones in each child's life.

As she felt her heart sinking lower and lower, she told herself, *you've got too much idle time these days. Nobody will feel so sad if they are workin' like they ought.*

Methodically, the long needle pierced the tender green beans until the bit of string was full then, hardly looking down, she wrapped the end of the string around a final bean ending the run. The split oak basket at her side was growing full and with each section of string she felt a little surer that her family would have food for the winter. She found she could not control her mind as easily as her needle for it raced ahead.

She tried to fight to control her thoughts until she realized that this might just be a chat with her Lord and there was so much she needed to lay before him.

As though turning the pages of a family scrap book, she reviewed each dear child and found that only in Roberta and Winnie could she see any fruit of the Holy Spirit. Roberta had walked the aisle at Campground church years ago, as so many young folks did. And in her life, Nadine saw a constant desire to be close to God. Winnie was very shy about her faith and many times she had talked quietly while they were working on one thing or the other. Her questions touched Nadine's heart and the tender spirit she revealed assured her this daughter was sensitive to the Lord's leading.

Both girls readily recognized the sin in their lives and as they came to understand, they reached eagerly for the supernatural saving power of Jesus Christ. Their lives were not easy, but Nadine was certain they were easier than the other children's because of God's leading in their hearts. When the family moved to Cliff Springs, Roberta allowed into her heart some bitterness toward their father. However, her letters now seemed filled with joy and she again spoke of living the way the Bible directed.

Not one of Nadine's boys showed any interest in a godly life. They wouldn't even pray over the family's meals and she doubted Jimmy or Jerry even knew where she kept the family Bible.

Lord, you know that I try never to run down Bill to any of his children. However, I believe my boys' salvation is hindered by the poor example of their father. There's no use in my denying it to you for I know you can see my heart. I guess that means I'm not truly respectful of my husband if this is in my heart. A godly woman respects her man and I've always thought I needed to teach both the boys and girls that. Please forgive me if I've focused so much on my husband that I've sacrificed my children. If these grown children can't see you in my heart and life then they won't have any chance of coming to know you.

The jingle of harness drew Nadine's eyes to the field as Harry led the horse into another row of corn and Jerry guided the single row cultivator through the short stalks. She couldn't help but admire the skill they had; it seemed that Jerry could farm like a grown man.

Lord, he is grown, isn't he? And he's smart; even with little schoolin' he can read and sum as well as anyone I've ever known. But I don't think I've ever seen him with the Bible in his hands.

Nadine blinked away a threatening tear just as Mary bounded up to her, basket in hand. "We're gonna' go find some blackberries. The boys said there's a thicket of 'em at the other end of this long field. We've got sugar enough for a pie, ain't we?"

"Child, you gotta' slow down. Yeah, we can make a pie if you can get enough berries. I'd enjoy a blackberry pie and I know your father would too." Nadine smiled down at the sweet girl. Mary was small for her age and that made her seem younger than Harry despite being two years his senior.

Mary ran off as quickly as she'd arrived pausing only slightly to draw Winnie along with her.

Nadine's hands had never slowed their work on the beans and the pile was steadily shrinking. Her mind turned back to its reflection as though the Lord himself drew her thoughts.

Lord, Mary seems so carefree and happy. But none of the boys have that air about them, not even Harry. How can a boy barely ten years old be so hard?

Remembering her babies brought a smile to her face and her hand to her swelling abdomen. She could still hear the first 'coos', the first time Harry said, "Mamamama". And she would never forget Roberta telling Lou "No" again and again.

Ah, it seems like it was just yesterday. And it makes me thankful to have a new baby on the way. This baby seems like a fresh start, but I will not give up on my other children. Father God, I will bring them before you so long as I have breath in my body. And even when I'm gone, I trust that those prayers will live on in you and that you will continue to draw my boys to you until everyone of them is saved from their sins.

Still, I'm asking right now that you would guide me to do better by this little one. You know I'll have him in church, the same as I've always done. But I see now that I need to speak more directly to him, or her, about his father. I guess I've kind of just ignored Bill's shortcomings. You know I've always prayed that he would be happier at home with his family. Now I'm asking that if we can't have Bill at home that Jimmy and Jerry will step up and be the father-figure this child needs just as they have stood in as head of household for me.

As the baby gave her a stout kick as though to remind her he was still there she said to him, "Little Lewis baby, we will give you a good life, I promise."

Chapter 21

Nadine looked around her table with a pang of sadness. She didn't have to look far to begin counting her blessings. Little Eddie came into the world perfectly healthy and sound and Nadine thought she'd recovered better than with any of her babies. Still, as she looked at the cooing baby in Mary's arms, she couldn't help but feel her family was shrinking.

The wind whistled through the un-insulated floor constantly reminding her of the freezing temperatures both Jimmy and Jerry faced as they worked in the logging woods. She smiled knowing that Naomi would be warm and would have food to eat this winter, even if she was worn to a frazzle with three babies under five years old. Nadine offered a quick prayer of thanks for the Tylers who she knew would take care of both their son and daughter-in-law. The same prayer begged care for Roberta whose letters sounded like she was living in the lap of luxury but Nadine feared her job could not be so grand.

Nadine knew that Jimmy and Jerry left home with nothing but bitter feelings toward their father and now she heard grumbling from Lou and Harry. They didn't dare speak directly to Bill, but neither held any respect for his decisions and they followed his orders only out of fear of the man and respect for their mother. Again her conscience sent a stabbing pain through her heart; surely as their mother she should have been able to make them love their father. Surely she had failed this family in some way.

Quietly, Nadine stepped away from the table and the buzzing of six voices. Solemnly looking out the tiny kitchen window, she tried to pour her heart out to God. But the words would not come.

Maybe that's been the problem all along, Lord. I keep trying to talk to you but I can never seem to get it out – no, I realize that you know my heart. Thank you for that promise Lord. Ah, I guess the difference is that I've not kept myself in Your Word and walking closely enough with you that I can know your heart and your will. Please forgive me for that. Do I still have any chance to change these older children? Surely there is hope for baby Eddie – he's so innocent and pure. I promise you Lord that I will teach him your word from this very day. Before he can even understand what I'm saying I will be speaking the gospel to him. If I have any power over this family at all, I will not allow this one to come up bitter and disgruntled.

But I can't just give up on Lou, Winnie, Mary or Harry. Give me wisdom to know how to guide them.

"Mother, why didn't you tell us it was snowing?" Mary's excited words interrupted her mother's sweet contemplation.

"Oh, it is snowing. My but it's early for a snow, don't you think so Bill?"

Bill Lewis scowled at the window and Nadine regretted bringing it to his attention. He had seemed somehow a little more satisfied here on the farm and she was dearly hoping he would stay home through the winter months. It was a comfort knowing he was here when she labored to deliver Eddie – although he offered no help, even sending Lou to bring the community midwife instead of going himself.

Nadine knew from many winters' experience that the falling snow made her husband feel trapped. She had spent countless nights walking the floor of whatever rented home they happened to be living in, wondering if he was safe in freezing temperatures – wondering if she'd ever see him again.

She had never shared these fears with her children. In fact, she had always put on an utterly positive face for them, assuring them that their father would be home in no time at all. And surely when he came home, he'd bring food and shoes and coats. The children never bothered to ask her why these promised provisions never arrived and she was thankful for she might have been tempted to lie to them in order to save-face for their father.

Bill called an end to breakfast by ushering the children out into the swirling snow to complete their chores. "When you get the stock fed, you need to turn to pulling the ears from them corn shocks. Sorry boys got it planted so late that we've only got three-quarters of the crop and the ears didn't cure good in the field. Maybe it's dried enough by now that we can feed the animals through a cold winter."

As the children filed out of the house, Nadine counted her blessings.

Thank you Lord that Jerry got a good, tight barn built before he left us. Now the children will at least have that shelter for most of their work.

Bill was pulling on his long duster as he said, "Coffee seemed a little weak this morning. Are we running low? I'll go down to Clarkrange and get a pound just in case this snow sticks."

Nadine smiled at him. "Surely it won't amount to much, after all it's still November."

Bill only grunted as he pulled his wide-brimmed hat down low on his forehead.

As the door slammed, Nadine tried to comfort herself that he was only going to Clarkrange. It was scarcely three miles so surely he'd be home for supper. She took the baby from Mary and shrugged away her fears. "Can you see after these dishes, Mary? I'll go feed little Eddie before he makes too big of a fuss."

Nadine had supper on the table and the children assembled before anyone noticed Bill had returned. He walked into the house, dropping a large cotton bag on Nadine's work table. It was far too big to contain only coffee and she looked into Bill's eyes seeking an explanation. Bill simply turned to take his place at the table.

Reaching into his shirt pocket, he handed a letter to Winnie. "Looks like it's from Roberta."

Winnie squealed and immediately tore into the envelope. The whole family was eager to hear from their sister and they insisted Winnie read the letter aloud.

Roberta always wrote as though her work and her new life were wonderful. And now she had found work for Winnie. She had befriended a young lady who worked in a store in Jamestown and she had been able to get her a place there. Winnie could stay with Roberta overnight then go on to Jamestown the next day. There were a couple of rooms above the store and Winnie could rent one of them.

Winnie's eyes sought out her mother, fear etched deeply in them. "Well that doesn't sound like going to stay with a family, does it? What do you think Mother?"

Nadine thought a great deal, but she carefully measured her words. Somehow she knew this would be a great opportunity for her daughter. Yet, Winnie was not as ambitious as Roberta and might struggle being completely out on her own. "Dear I think it sounds like a great opportunity."

She didn't know how to mention how very young she thought Winnie was to be leaving home. Of course, at thirteen, Nadine heard of lots of girls finding work and even some who would marry by fourteen although Nadine resolved to never allow one of her daughter to wed so young.

Winnie clamped her teeth tightly on her lower lip and walked silently from the room with Roberta's letter still in her hand.

As she cleared the table and made the kitchen ready to serve its double duty as the boys' bedroom, Nadine again turned her mind to talking with the Lord. *Lord, it seems like my table is emptying quickly. I know that Winnie will go to work in this store – the girls aren't quite so hard-hearted toward Bill as their brothers are, but they naturally long to have pretty things. At least this winter there will be food, or so it seems. Surely Bill won't go off on any trips when it's already gotten cold and snowy. But if she's working, I could be sure Winnie would have food and shelter. This might even be a chance for her to meet a nice young man*

Thinking of husbands for her daughters turned her thoughts back to her sons. *Lord, I don't know this Austin family very well. And Jimmy's married one daughter and Jerry seems bent on marrying their Vera – I wish I could know they've had a Christian upbringing. You know that my boys will need strong, godly women behind them.*

At some point in the cleaning process, Winnie had made her way back into the kitchen and settled on the bed in the corner. She was still so deeply in thought that Nadine didn't even ask for her help with the dishes. Mary still held Eddie near the cookstove. It was the only source of heat in the house and usually kept a comfortable temperature in the kitchen although it took a lot of work to keep a fire going in the tiny firebox. However, as the wind kicked up, the persistent draft allowed a chill to settle over the house. Eddie was never far from the stove.

Nadine turned to the doorway in the front room which doubled as parlor and the boys' bedroom. "Lou, Harry, will one of you please dump the water for me?" Stepping back to the kitchen, within arm's reach of her youngest son, Nadine took him from Mary, "Mary if you will dry the dishes for me, I'll take care of Eddie's diaper and feed him."

Quiet and obedient as usual, Mary did as she was asked and brought a genuine smile to her mother's face. *Thank you Lord for this little helper I have in Mary. Thank you for each of my children, Naomi and Jimmy included. Please heal the wounds in this family. And I promise you, so long as you give me breath in my body, I will speak more directly to them, I will speak about you clearly and often. I will do anything you lead me to do to see my children saved.*

Chapter 22

It was a hard winter. Everyone agreed; everyone talked about it. It snowed and snowed and snowed and when it wasn't snowing, the temperatures refused to warm many degrees above freezing. By January, everyone on the mountain longed for springtime.

As Nadine wrapped a woolen scarf around her shoulders, she wondered if the house really was colder without as many bodies living in it, or was that just her imagination.

The log kitchen had long since given up much if its chinking and despite the children's constant efforts to stuff newspaper or rags into the cracks, the wind found a way to blow in and wage war with the big iron stove. Mostly the stove was winning – at least, no one was showing signs of frostbite. Nadine smiled at the extreme thought. This wasn't the worst house the family had ever wintered in and they'd always survived.

Nadine was increasingly convinced that survival was by God's grace alone. She looked at little Mary patiently sitting as close to the stove as she dared and holding the baby. Nadine remembered winters with her other babies lying on a pallet by the stove. But she was sure the constant draft would be the death of baby Eddie and she didn't want to chance it. She was determined this child would grow up in the center of God's word and will. She had great plans for him and wouldn't let him freeze before she had the chance to see those plans fulfilled.

Lord, that's wrong too. Please forgive me. He is yours and I know that it's your plan that matters in his life. But I commit to you that I will do my part to have him in church and to protect him from the life that has filled his brothers with hate.

Church - the very thought brought a thin smile. She hadn't been able to make the trip to Campground in over a month and she doubted anyone else had either. Everyone seemed thankful to make it to the barn to milk and care for their stock.

She patted the letter from Winnie that she still carried in the deep pocket of her apron. It reassured her that Roberta truly was working for a good family that cared for her and that Winnie had safely made the trip to Jamestown and settled into a shared room above the store where she worked. It was good there were other girls staying there, Winnie was really too young to be completely on her own. As she did every time anything reminded her of the girls, Nadine said a quick prayer for God to lead them to godly husbands.

Bill scoffed at her mourning the girls' departure. He'd said, "You act like they've gone to meet their maker. They ain't, they've only gone to Jamestown. And by-Jingo, they've left us with all the work to do. Should be here clearin' the fields and I've a half a mind to go get them soon's the weather's good 'nough to be in the fields."

Nadine ignored his threats. He didn't even seem to know where they'd gone. After all, only Winnie was in Jamestown; Roberta was only half so far away in Grimsley. There was no need arguing with him though, and Nadine did try to avoid arguing with her husband.

While Bill seemed not to miss his children, he leaned ever harder on those who remained under his roof. Lou in particular was suffering as his father demanded more and more from him and instead of treating the sixteen year old like a man, he persisted in demeaning Lou every chance he had.

Although he'd never say it directly to her, Nadine knew of Lou's growing unrest. She heard the bits of talk between Lou and Harry; and Mary occasionally shared more than her brother meant for her to. He knew if he left home now he would have to go work with his brothers or hire on at someone's farm. Neither of those options was particularly appealing to him. And he also felt responsible for the care of his mother, as well as young Harry for he knew if he left all of his father's abuse would fall on the younger boys. Just the thought of it caused Nadine to unconsciously begin wringing her hands.

When Christmas Day arrived, it was beautiful as the mountain was blanketed with fresh white snow and the wind calmed for the day. Jerry came home for the delicious meal Nadine and Mary prepared. Winnie had written that she would be spending the day with Roberta. Even as Nadine asked the family to bow their heads to pray, she saw Bill eyeing the snow-covered road as though he were calculating how treacherous it would be to make one of his trips. There was no use in asking him to pray for his family for his heart wasn't even with them.

She looked to Jerry, thankful to have him home if only for a day. However, something in his red-rimmed eyes and sallow complexion told her he was not fit to bring the family before the Lord. In the end, she led the prayer herself and silently added a plea that her sons would come to walk closely to God.

By New Year's Bill had left with some excuse no one could even remember. He didn't return at dark and only Nadine paced with worry. After two day's absence, Lou came looking for Nadine after breakfast.

"There's no reason to keep watching that road. You know it may be months before we see him again."

She smiled at him. He had grown up so much over the last two years and now he would serve as her head of household until Bill returned. "I know, but it scares me just a little when your father is traveling in the winter."

Ignoring any concern for his father, Lou wanted to explain that he'd been thinking how the family might survive the remaining winter months. "We still have a good herd of hogs. He only sold the fattest ones, no doubt thinking to hold some for the late winter months when folks will pay more for fresh meat. But we can be selling those right away. That would provide some cash money. And Mary and Harry will help me butcher one for the family to eat."

"Oh Lou, I don't know that your father would want you to…"

She had no chance to finish her thought, no chance to urge him to respect his father. Lou practically spit the words out, "As he would say, 'By-Jingo' I'll not have fat hogs in the barn and a hollow belly. We'll eat before we line his pockets." He turned on his heel and stomped out of the house.

Nadine winced at the slamming door. She knew he meant her no disrespect; Lou was always respectful of his mother.

With his older brothers gone, Lou cared well for his family, ensuring there was food on their table and managing to have a little cash money for those things they simply had to buy. He even got shoes for Mary and Harry, saying that they wouldn't be able to help with the work if they were laid up with frostbite.

At the first hint of spring, Lou had little Harry in front of the team while he wrestled the plow along furrows too long left fallow. In fact, that's how Bill found them when he ambled across the field as though he'd spoken with them just this morning.

"Harry if you can't lead that nag in a straight line just turn her lose. A wild horse would plow a straighter row than you two."

Harry looked back at his brother; the criticism from his father stung the little boy but his greater concern was the crimson color creeping up Lou's neck. Harry turned back to his father expecting him to direct them how to better turn the ground into a managed cropland.

Bill took the last steps through the rough weeds. He'd been faced with a choice of walking through freshly plowed ground or unplowed, weedy turf. Neither choice presented an easy walk. Now, he was slightly out of breath despite the slow pace he set. He turned his questions to Lou. "What made you think it was time to plow? Signs ain't right and I don't guess we'll raise a thing here. You ought to be splitting fence rails instead of wasting your time out here."

Lou was gripping the plow handle so tightly that his knuckles were turning white. "Well Sir, I had to hitch the horse to plow the garden anyway."

"Garden! If you let that woman – or any woman – plan your days, you'll never profit."

Lou tried to take a deep breath and swallow his words but they threatened to gag him. He opened his mouth and years of pent-up emotion fairly gushed out. He began with a stream of foul language that made Harry look quickly around lest Mother should hear. "You know what? You make me sick always blathering about *profit*. Sure you turn a profit, then you let your family fairly starve to death. You leave in the dead of winter and never wonder whether we've survived or not. Mother wants the garden plowed so she can maybe raise enough food to feed her kids."

Lou only paused to take a breath but Bill took the opportunity to respond. "You look fit enough after the winter."

Lou's eyes widened and seemed to bulge from his face, "No thanks to you. Mother and Mary sat beside the stove the livelong winter for fear of laying the baby down in a house that's got more draft than a big fireplace. I don't know where you've been but you might as well have stayed there. We were doing just fine in Cliff Springs without you. Now we've made it through the winter without you so I reckon me and Harry can get a crop in and get this family through the summer without you."

Bill spit his chew of tobacco on the ground and wiping his mouth with the back of his hand he slowly turned toward the barn. "Gonna' take a look at my hogs. Bet you've let them fall off considerable in the cold weather."

Chapter 23

Nadine happened to be looking out her kitchen window as Bill stepped from the barn. She didn't know that he had come home and her heart swelled at the sight of him. However, his deep scowl immediately warned her he was displeased with something and fear chased away her moment of joy. She pondered, *Oh my, what have we done wrong now?*

Bill looked from side to side, seeing nothing. The rage boiled within him as he mentally calculated how much money Lou had stolen from him. Surely it was theft. He left a sound and growing herd of hogs and came home just two months later to a depleted herd. For the briefest moment his mind reasoned perhaps some disease had stricken them, killing off the missing animals. Bill immediately dismissed that thought. He was sure Lou had stolen from him and he would immediately confront his defiant son. He would not have a thief under his roof.

Bill looked across the field and watched as Lou and Harry diligently worked the single horse up and down the field, rich black soil turning up behind the plow. He decided to let them finish the day's plowing – might as well get the day's work out of Lou before he set him on the road. Bill turned toward the house hoping Nadine would have the coffeepot hot and waiting for him.

He took his seat at the head of the table and that is where Lou and Harry found him when hunger and thirst finally drove them from their plowing.

Lou was teaching Harry as they walked through the open doorway. "The horse needs to rest even more than we do. Remember, she's pulling that plow through unbroken sod. So even if you feel like you could work a little longer, you have to take care of your stock."

Nadine took the moment to make a spiritual application. All winter she'd jumped at every opportunity to speak the name of Jesus in her home and to her children. "That's good teaching Lou. It's biblical you know, Proverbs tells us that a righteous man cares for his animals."

As Lou respectfully listened to his mother, he realized Bill was at the table. Despite his esteem for his mother, he couldn't bite back the snide comment as he looked directly at his father, "Does it say the same about people?"

Nadine dropped her head momentarily, realizing she had opened the door for her son's bitterness to spill out.

Bill ignored Lou's comment, he had his own agenda. "Did yu'ns finish plowin' that field?"

Harry answered, eager to share the lesson Lou had just been teaching him. "No Sir, Jewel was a'needin' a rest. See, she's been pullin' that heavy plow. And the good book tells us to take care of our animals."

Again, Bill ignored his younger son. "Lou I seen the hogs, counted 'em you know. I know you've been sellin' 'em off through the winter. I'll expect you to be handin' that profit over to me now."

Lou's eyes popped open wide, "Profit? Don't you guess we ate that *profit?*" He fairly spit the word 'profit' every time he spoke it.

Bill responded with a mouthful of curses, causing Nadine to bury her head in her hands.

Lou glanced at his mother, at once heartbroken to see her crying and infuriated at the man who would cause it without flinching. He lit into his father as none of his brothers had ever dared before. "I guess somebody's got to keep this family from plumb starving to death. Don't you realize that Jimmy's been doin' just that for years? He tramped through the woods trying to kill whatever game he could find. And do you suppose that every chicken he said he found caught in the fence got there on its own? No, he knew we had nothing to eat and he brought something home. Even with everything he could do, we've had little enough. Barefoot in the dead of winter, Mother washin' every night 'cause we had but one pair of overalls. And you dare speak of *profit?* I just wish you could tell me why it is that you can walk away from your family for months at a time and leave them with no money and no means of feeding and clothing themselves? How can you do that to Mother?"

Lou's lungs screamed at him and he realized he'd barely breathed during the whole tirade.

Bill waited out his sons fit of words, nearly enjoying the spunk this one showed. He had always been disappointed with his boys, do-less bunch that they were. He thought they never had the gumption to say 'boo' to a goose. And the lot of them living under his roof and letting him take care of them until they were way past grown. Why, Bill remembered he'd left home when he was barely fourteen years old and Jimmy hadn't bothered to go until he was past twenty. Now this one had found some nerve. Maybe he would leave home on his own, for Bill was certainly planning to put him out for the crime of stealing his hogs.

He could see that Lou's fountain of wrath had run dry and he seized the moment, "If you are quite finished… I don't see how the four of you could have eaten *four* hogs. There is money here and I mean to find it."

Bill stood as though he would search the house, Lou moved toe-to-toe with his father. Bill Lewis stood only five foot six, but his girth and pride tended to make one think he was bigger. And the bully and bluster personality kept most men from troubling him. Today Lou was undeterred.

He did not yell as his father was inclined to do. He spoke in such a low, controlled voice that he fairly mesmerized every ear in the room. "There is but little money in this house and yes, whatever is here came from the sale of those hogs. But you will not touch it. Mother has a bit of coffee and a few pounds of flour and meal, some sugar and salt. That's what's left of your *profit*. There's a side of pork left that will put meat on the table for two or three meals. After that, your children will either do without meat or I'll find something in the woods to kill. Even if you were sharing the table with us, I have rarely known you to hunt for the food you would eat. But you won't be sharing that table. We don't need you and we do not want you here."

Nadine gasped. She had said nothing, in fact she had not moved since the exchange began. Now, she must step in, must find a way to smooth this over. She could not have Lou speaking so disrespectfully to his father. *Oh Lord, if I've failed to teach him the ten commandments, how can he ever learn the bigger, deeper lessons you have for him?*

Bill had been a gambler for years now. And, he'd taken many a hefty pot from men both weak and strong. If he'd learned anything he'd learned when to walk away and right now he judged he must walk away from Lou.

Without another word, he picked up the hat and duster he'd thrown over a chair. Placing the hat on his head he looked for the briefest moment at his wife and then stepped out the open doorway into the noonday sun. The family stood motionless; in a moment, Bill's tuneless whistle could be heard slowly fading away.

Chapter 24

Bill ambled slowly out the front path that led to the roadway. He stood for a moment looking first to the East then Westward. Usually when he began one of his trips he had already spent hours mulling over the direction he wanted to take and people he might want to see; but above all he left knowing his purpose for the journey. Today, however, he'd planned to rest, allowing Nadine to care for him as her nurturing nature caused her to care for everyone in her house. Lou had abruptly changed the plan.

Bill was an expert at maintaining a bluff and he never dreamed one of his sons would ever call that bluff. When Lou stood up to him and accused him of neglecting his family, something in the boy's eyes told Bill it was time to walk away from this particular game.

As he walked, he thought. In fact, his head was spinning as it rarely did.

When the urge to move-on called him away from his home or his work, no one ever asked him to stay. Well, no one except Nadine, and she never begged. In fact as he thought over the past twenty years of his life, he wondered if he was ever really wanted anywhere. He couldn't help but think of Ann, she had always wanted him with her.

Ann, you took everything when you died.

117

Bill shook his head – he couldn't start talking to himself much less his dead wife. Yet somehow he couldn't stop his mind as it rolled through memories and imagined what might have been had Ann survived the birth of their son. Oh he couldn't blame Jimmy, he never had blamed him. Ann was sick with the consumption before she had him, probably even before she conceived him. Looking back on it, Bill could see that she didn't have as much energy as before. She seemed to barely get over one cold before she took another one, and they always seemed to settle in her chest leaving her coughing for weeks. Ann dismissed it, saying that her family all had weak lungs and colds just ran that way with them. Bill was young and so in love with his wife that he would have believed a green sky was perfectly normal if she said it and gave him that tender, sweet smile.

Ann, you always wanted me at home with you. I remember driving hogs to Kentucky and you practically begging me to stay. I wonder now if you knew you were dying and you didn't want to be alone. But you weren't alone my dear – in the end I sat and held your hand until you drew your last breath. It seems like that was my last breath of life too 'cause there's been no joy in anything since then.

As though Ann, or some spirit, spoke in his ear Bill questioned, *Why couldn't you find any happiness with Nadine? She took you and your two children when she was young and beautiful. She surely had many beaus to choose from.*

Bill stopped and looked back toward the old, dilapidated house where he'd left his wife and four of their children. He was too far away to see the house; he could just make out the tops of the trees that surrounded it. He stood there watching, as though he might see Nadine, as though she would still be that beautiful young woman.

Then his mind turned to Mercy. She was so different from Nadine. Mercy was so small, when her father handed her to Bill, he'd thought she was only a child.

Well, she was practically a child. Just sixteen I think.

Bill had never really regretted accepting Mercy from her father. After all, he'd made the bet fair and square. And Mercy had worked hard to serve Bill as her husband, but somehow Bill always knew that it was to honor her father and not him. Still there had never been any real joy in their marriage, nothing like he'd shared with Ann.

Again, the voice in his head challenged him, *How could that marriage have anything that your marriage to Ann had – Mercy didn't even know you when she married you, much less did she love you. Does she love you now?*

Bill pondered that question for a moment and remembered the look in her eyes as he said goodbye to her just a few weeks ago. Then he realized, far from loving him, she didn't even respect him. *Why is that?* He pondered.

He reasoned with himself that he made good money. In fact, every venture he'd undertaken in the past few years had been profitable with some being extremely profitably. He tapped his pocket, reassured by the roll of bills he felt there. His fingers registered the fine weave of his pants and as he looked down at them he noted the gleam of soft leather boots that had been polished just yesterday by a boy at the general store.

Simultaneously, his mind flashed visions of both Nadine in her faded cotton dress and Mercy in a worn shift made of homespun cloth. He shrugged his shoulders, wondering what these women had to do with how well he was dressed. Surely they realized how much he had paid for the clothes. *Well of course they know, haven't you cautioned them time and again to use care when they are washing them? You've told them these clothes can't be treated like the other rags they scrub out.*

Bill walked and walked, his thoughts driving him onward heedless of the direction. The sun slipped toward the western horizon but he did not notice. The day faded to dusk, his eyes adjusted and he kept walking.

Bill talked himself out of worrying about Lou's unspoken threats. In fact, he began to ask himself why he hadn't ridden one of the horses. He dismissed the questions of whether his families missed him or wanted him around. In fact, he began to wonder if this would be a good time to sell the farm.

Even before he saw the decimated herd of swine, he'd realized that this farm was not bringing the joy he thought he'd find. It was nothing like the farms he tended in his youth when he'd been overfilled with joy. No, it would be best to try to sell it and turn a profit. The boys had the fields looking good and with the addition of the barn Jerry had built he could command a much better price than what he paid.

When he finally came to his decision, the hour had grown quite late and the road very dark. He stopped to figure out where he was but he was surrounded by dense woodland. He couldn't remember when he'd last passed a farm and looking behind he could see no sign of a lamp in a window. Trying to think back on what he'd seen earlier in the day, he realized that he was headed toward Monterey and this must be the big woods. How long had he been in this forest? He wouldn't come out of it before he reached the edge of town. Now he must decide whether to keep tripping along the road or make himself as comfortable as possible at base of a tree for the night.

He looked around; the night was warm, muggy even. He'd certainly been out in worse conditions. No, he had a plan now and he would continue on his way into Monterey. He would make it there before the public house closed and he might even be able to do some business before the morning.

Chapter 25

Nadine occupied her familiar spot peering out the little kitchen window which afforded her an easterly view of The Monterey Road. She watched the passersby, whenever there were any. On a couple of occasions she'd even seen an automobile chugging along. As she watched today, her hands always busy, the road was clear but out of the corner of her eye she saw movement on the path leading to the house. She leaned close to the window and nearly gasped when she realized Bill was striding rather quickly toward the house. He walked with purpose as he rarely did when walking toward his family. She quickly tried to count how many days he'd been gone – they were so few that she hadn't yet begun to keep track.

In a moment the kitchen door crashed open; Nadine jumped despite expecting him. She tried to look deep into his eyes to read whether he was angry, but saw no emotion at all within them.

"Where's that boy?" he demanded.

She was sure it was Lou he wanted, after all the last words Bill heard in this room were those Lou hurled toward him.

"Lou and Harry are out in the barn, I think."

"Mary!" he yelled. "Mary get down to the barn and bring them boys up here."

Mary had been in the front bedroom with little Eddie. She scurried through the kitchen without even looking at her father.

121

She took no time to ask why or to greet the man.

Nadine quietly excused herself to go ensure Eddie had been left in a safe position. She was sorely tempted to just stay in the bedroom for she did not look forward to the encounter between her husband and their son. But she realized she must be there, if only to take advantage of any opportunity to keep the peace among her family.

Mary completed her errand quickly and by the time Nadine left a dry and napping Eddie carefully placed in the center of the girl's bed, Lou, Mary and Harry were entering the kitchen.

Lou walked a pace ahead of his siblings, his face set with fierce determination. His mouth opened to speak, or shout, the moment he crossed the threshold. However, Bill did not give him a chance.

"Are them horses shod?" he asked anyone who could answer. "Get one of 'em saddled. I ain't a'walkin' when I leave here this time."

Harry nodded his head. This was a chore he could easily do.

Bill continued, expecting his family to eagerly hear and attend to his every demand. "Got some fella from down in the Sequatchie Valley gonna' buy this place. We're a'goin' to the court house tomorrow mornin' so yu'ns will have to get cleared out right quick."

Crimson red crept up Lou's neck and his eyes held a wild look. He clenched his fists so tightly they turned white. Nadine stepped forward to prevent Lou and Bill exchanging blows. She wasn't sure who would win such a match and she had no intention of finding out.

Bill too saw the anger rising but seemed unconcerned. He turned to continue speaking to Mary and Harry.

Lou cut him off short, "How dare you march in here after we've worked the whole summer to get this place ready for winter."

"By-jingo, I dare 'cause it's my own place."

"You own it." Lou's words hissed through teeth clamped too tightly for language. "Well, you don't OWN me or anybody else in this room. We'll never again be dependent on anything you OWN."

Turning to the rest of the family and taking charge as he never had before Lou directed them, "Get packin'. I'll go find us a place to live that he can't touch. This is the last time I work day and night to make a place fit to live in only to have it sold or traded right out from under me."

With that, Lou was gone. Nadine feared she would never see her son again; however, she did as he'd asked and began packing. Quietly, she asked Harry to bring the wagon up to the house.

Harry asked, "How we gonna' pull it if Father's takin' one of the horses?"

"Oh, I hadn't thought of that. Well, wait till Lou gets back, he'll know what to do."

When Lou returned it was nearly dark. Nadine saw him riding on a very slow-moving mule which he put into the barn. He walked into the house and surveyed the kitchen from the doorway.

"He left right after you."

Lou went to the little wash stand by his the bed and bathed his face and arms as he talked to his mother. "I've rented the little house of Frank Miller's just down the road. He's goin' up north to look for work; said he was leavin' by the end of the week but he'll let you and the baby sleep in the front room till they get packed up. Borrowed his old mule too. Wish I could buy it but there's just no way. We'll return it to his pa when we get our house plunder moved."

"How did you manage? What will we use to pay rent?"

Lou slumped into a straight-back chair, "Went to see Jimmy first. He'll help us when we need it. I know Jerry will too, 'cept I didn't get to see him 'cause he's gone with a load of logs. Can you b'lieve he's drivin' a truck that's big enough to pull them logs up out of the Baldwin Gulf?"

Nadine shook her head, stopping for a moment to wonder at her son's accomplishments after such a short time working in the log-woods. Then she let out a breath she felt she'd been holding all afternoon. She realized that while Bill had constantly moved the family from one place to another, she'd never been without a home of some sort. This had been a scary afternoon for her.

The next days, even weeks, would be a blur whenever Nadine tried to recall them. She and the children were welcomed into the

Miller's home as though they were their own family. The boys seemed happy bunking in the barn for about ten days before Frank Miller declared they were ready to head up north.

Of course Harry mentioned to his mother a number of times, "That barn ain't nothin' like the one Jerry built down the road. Boy, that sure was a fine barn – tight, why I don't think there'd ever be a blowin' rain that would get through them walls. But this barn will do us just fine I reckon."

Winnie quickly accepted the position Roberta had found for her in Jamestown and after that Nadine saw neither of the girls very often but they wrote faithfully and she was confident they were doing well and both seemed poised to marry into the same, respectable family.

There was no land with this house for the fields around it were still tended by Frank's father. They had only a little garden plot and the whole family worked to make it produce every bit that it could.

Jimmy and Jerry faithfully helped with bills and ensured there was always food in the little house. Harry found work whenever he could, and with each passing year he was able to earn a little more money. So the family was getting along very well, until the war.

Chapter 26

Eddie handed his mother the letters he'd picked up at Peter's Store as Nadine stepped onto the little porch surrounded by bright flowers and took her seat on a woven rag rug that served to cover the rough chair. She smiled, appreciating the tranquil sanctuary she'd been able to create here. After sixteen years in the little rented house, the plantings had established themselves and flourished. Never, since leaving her father's house, had she had even half that much time to make a home in one place.

Her mind flashed back to the day they moved; she inhaled deeply of the honeysuckle that wrapped itself around one end of her porch and drew her mind back to the present. *No need to dwell on what's happened all those years ago.*

She looked at the letters in her hand and seeing the postmarks, she took a moment to pray. Two letters from her boys. Harry, stationed stateside in Maine, and Lou who was somewhere overseas – the Army was so secretive about those things. There was a moment's joy every time she saw the AP/FPO address identifying one of them. Three boys in service, it seemed like such a sacrifice. At least they'd left the youngest of the three within the relative safety of American borders. Still she stopped to praise God every time because that meant that at least a few weeks ago her boy was well enough to write. The feel of the third envelope told her it was the government check paying her the allotment Lou and Harry had each setup to send home. Jerry was also serving overseas but felt his money should be sent to his wife Vera, and Nadine certainly agreed.

Lou's letter opened with questions about her and Eddie's welfare. Lou always wanted to ensure that the allotment had been received and that it was sufficient for them. All three of the boys seemed to take comfort knowing that their service was not only helping to keep America free, but it also helped to feed and house their mother.

Eddie skipped the steps and hopped onto the porch, dragging a ladder back chair close to his mother.

Nadine smiled at her baby. She was so proud of him, and she knew his brothers and sisters were too. "You are just in time. I've barely started reading these. Will you read them to me? I just love to hear you read aloud."

Handing off the letters, Nadine again closed her eyes. She allowed Eddie's strong, young voice to penetrate her mind and praised God for this product of the education he had received. Again thanks to his brothers, Eddie's childhood had been stable enough for him to be in school every term and they even found a way to buy the books he needed. As proud as she felt of Eddie, hearing him read broke her heart for her older boys who had never had the same opportunities for schooling.

As Eddie read, Nadine imagined she could see Europe as Lou described it. Somehow she had always thought it would be drabber, less exciting than Lou found it. Yet he described beautiful flowers, green fields and homes finer than any she'd ever imagined. Eddie read on, "I'm hoping we'll be home before long. We're always thinking it can't last much longer." Any explanation of Lou's thoughts was caught by the censor's blade.

Harry's letter was shorter. He wasn't quite as enamored with the great state of Maine as his brother was with Europe. Harry talked of late springs and longing to be home plowing; he said so little that Nadine knew he was purposely keeping the details of his life from her. What she didn't know was why and with every letter she implored the Lord to protect him. Were the conditions so bad that he didn't dare worry her? Or were his Air Force friends such that he did not want his mother to know about them? Either way, she knew he needed divine protection.

The only joy Nadine saw when her boys were drafted was the possibility that war might draw them to God. Unfortunately, no note came from any of them declaring newfound faith. Still their mother prayed.

Eddie sat quietly with the open letters on his lap. Whether he too prayed for the distant family or just respected his mother's heavenly pleas, the comfortable silence lingered.

Chapter 27

Mercy didn't even try to catch the banging door as she came in from the garden, arms loaded with baskets of produce. Bill napped on the new chair and ottoman he'd brought home a few weeks ago. Mercy looked at the new furniture, feeling slightly disgusted. She certainly enjoyed the comfort of the tightly stuffed cushions when she allowed herself to relax on them for a few minutes at day's end. But whenever Bill was home, he seemed to always be found there. And he was home a lot these days.

The change had caught Mercy off-guard. She thought back to the first time he left; it was six months before he returned that time and he came no more frequently for the next ten years. Then suddenly he showed up one day, just as he had so many times over the years. He stayed a while and left without explanation. But this time he was back in just a few weeks. And he began staying longer and longer. He still seemed to have money when he came home and he'd brought things into the home that she certainly appreciated, like the furniture and an ice box and until rationing began to affect everyone, he'd even brought home fruit and candy a few times. Since America entered the war, they were thankful to have the vegetables she could raise and the game her now grown nephews provided.

Mercy shook her head asking herself, *How long ago was that? I wonder why he started coming home so much more. He certainly didn't seem to care anymore for his daughter or his wife than he ever did. Tsula was so small then, not more than six years old.*

The house was so quiet without Tsula that Mercy thought she ought to be happy to have Bill here. But somehow she couldn't muster that emotion with him. And he certainly wasn't happy with her. He complained about the house – that's when he brought in the furniture. He complained about the water, said it tasted stale all the time – that's when he brought home the ice box. He complained about her cooking but always managed to devour anything she put on the table.

In the early days Mercy had worried that he stayed away because he was so dissatisfied with her and everything she did. However, as the years rolled by, she began to realize this man couldn't be made happy with anything. Therefore, she had long since decided not to worry about his happiness. She, on the other hand, found happiness in so many aspects of her life.

She smiled at the thought of Tsula in her starched, white nurse's uniform. Mercy feared the sixteen-year-old was too young to be away from home, but reminded herself that she was married when she was Tsula's age. And she was sure Tsula would marry soon too. She still corresponded with and always talked about the young soldier she'd brought home for Mercy to meet. The soldier stood proud in his neatly pressed uniform, garrison cap cocked slightly to the right side of his head. He had stopped trying to pronounce Tsula's name and shortened it to Sue. Mercy always remembered Bill refusing to use their daughter's Cherokee name and instead calling her "Sulie". However, the girl didn't mind the nickname her beau used, and many of her friends adopted it as well.

Tsula made the trip back to Strawberry Plains quite often, walking from the depot to their little house outside town. Despite her youth, she had realized that her father was home much more than when she was a child and she didn't like it. The older Tsula grew, the more outspoken she became to her mother about this man. She didn't like him and she didn't mind saying it.

Mercy urged her precious daughter not to speak ill of her father. She tried to teach her that even a poor father still deserved the honor demanded of the fifth commandment. This would always quiet Tsula for Mercy had routinely taught her from the Bible. Still, the issue kept coming up.

When Tsula met Harvey she couldn't help thinking of her own father and tried to keep herself from falling in love with the young man. Only when she confessed this struggle to her mother did Mercy finally tell her the whole story of how she married Bill Lewis.

Mercy thought this would help her daughter better understand why she had humbly accepted Bill's treatment through the years. However, Tsula responded, "Oh Aluli, you don't have to stay with him now. Your father, my Adudi is long gone and he would not be dishonored if you divorced Bill Lewis."

Mercy closed her eyes in a moment's quick prayer for divine guidance. "Tsula, it's not just my Doda that I long to honor. Don't you see that by honoring the marriage vows I honor God, even if your father has not respected his family?"

Tsula left that evening without really understanding her mother's heart and Mercy realized more clearly than ever that she had failed to truly teach Tsula about God's love. With this realization, Mercy began to question whether she had blamed God all these years. She resolved to spend some time alone in prayer and work through that troubling question.

The talk with her mother opened Tsula's heart to Harvey and their love began to grow despite the long distance between Knoxville, Tennessee and Harvey's unknown location in the Pacific. Tsula wrote every week, writing a little each day and posting the letter only when it was almost too thick for the envelope. Harvey's letters arrive sporadically and Tsula seemed to live for them. By this method they were planning a wedding and their life together.

Mercy took heart that Tsula was not so wounded by her father's absences through the years that she would not have a family of her own. She had tried very hard to show her daughter what a good and happy family life would be like by keeping her close to the Hawks. Her nieces and nephews were mostly grown now too and many of them had moved to other places to find work just as Tsula had. Still, Mercy was hopeful that after being so close while growing up the cousins would stay in touch with each other.

While she reminisced, Mercy had sorted the vegetables, putting the nicest ones in a basket to take to sell and cleaning those she would cook for supper. She stirred the fire and set a skillet to heat, noting that Bill was moving in his sleep and would certainly wake in time to eat.

She marveled that the house seemed just as empty and lonely when he was in it as it did when he was gone. Maybe she would walk over to see her sister-in-law after supper. It was a nice evening and the ladies often visited after supper. Until Tsula and Harvey would give her grandchildren, this would be her life and she was resolved to be content in it.

Chapter 28

V-E Day! The radio announced it, the papers lauded it, all of the world celebrated.

Nadine's quiet world wasn't racked with the cheers and fireworks that resounded around Trafalgar or Times Square, but the joy was no less real. Surely now her boys would be coming home. Of course, everyone was quick to remember that the battle still raged in the Pacific – surely, she thought, none of her boys would be sent there after giving so much of themselves to the European campaign. Would the Army send Harry to fight the Japanese since he had been in the US throughout the war?

Nadine could not even consider that. Today was a day of celebration around the globe and she would not allow her fears to darken that.

She carefully guarded the money that Lou and Harry sent from their paychecks, however today she sent Eddie to Clarkrange with their carefully watched ration card for sugar – today, they would have a cake. After all, she reasoned, she would soon be cooking for the returning heroes so she must be in good practice to make some special foods. She smiled at her own ability to rationalize an indulgence.

Within days she had a letter from Harry, and shortly after that Vera came with word from Jerry. His company would be boarding a troop ship within the week and sailing for home. Vera and Nadine embraced and cried and laughed; it was a surreal moment for they'd begun to fear their prayers would never be answered. Jerry was drafted first and he had been gone for three, long years.

Nadine waited for word from Lou. He was serving as a medic and was still very much needed; it would be another month before it was his turn to sail for home. Thankfully, there was no indication that he would be required to serve in the Pacific theatre.

As her boys returned home, rationing eased, and jobs were available, the family settled into a comfortable routine. Roberta and Winnie were married to two brothers whose family owned a big store in Jamestown. Roberta and her husband Lenny moved to Crossville where the Wallace family was opening a new store. Nadine was thrilled to know her daughters were married to good men who would undoubtedly care for and love them. Both of her sons-in-law had cars that enabled them to visit very often. In fact Winnie's husband, Emmett, was teaching Eddie to drive and they were encouraging him to come live with them and work in the new store.

She was thrilled to see each of her boys looking to their future. She had hoped that the struggles and victories from the war years would change them, make them thankful to the God that protected them and cause them to focus on their blessings instead of the evil around them. They were indeed changed but not altogether as she'd hoped.

Lou and Harry found every bar and tavern within driving distance, for Lou came home driving a nice automobile purchased with his mustering-out bonus. They worked hard, and continued to give her money to support the household, but they spent every remaining penny in those drinking establishments. Nadine walked the floor at night praying, begging God to draw them home, to draw them toward himself.

It wasn't long before Jimmy and Jerry began talking about moving their mother out of the rented house. Even though there was still much work available in the northern states, they feared the Millers would return home and want to move back into their house. And everyone felt it would be better to own the house rather than continue to rent.

Roberta and Lenny had recently built a new home on a large piece of land in nearby Crossville. They offered Nadine a portion of that land. Jerry had been hiring on with local carpenters and found that he truly had a gift for the work. It was decided; Jerry and Lou would do the building, Jimmy and Harry would help them buy the materials. Eddie would be expected to help Jerry and Lou; he would stay with Roberta and Lenny while the work was being done and whenever he couldn't work on the house, they would use him in the new store.

The children had fallen into the habit of making decisions on Nadine's behalf without really even consulting her. The smallest part of her wanted to argue, but they were taking such good care of her that she refused to complain. It seems that after watching so many years of their mother's total submission to their father, they felt she wasn't capable of deciding things on her own. Nadine's only concern about this perception was her failure to make her children understand just why she followed their father without complaint or argument. If only she could have succeeded in winning Bill Lewis to the Lord – maybe then the children would have seen the value in her sacrifices.

He may change yet. She'd told herself that a million times over the years. Even now, when she had neither seen nor heard of Bill for more than a decade, she prayed for his salvation. She longed to hear that he had come to a saving knowledge of Jesus Christ even if he still did not come home to her. She wondered if the boys would accept him if he came humbly, confessing his sins. She smiled as The Parable of The Prodigal son came to mind; how perfectly that could apply to Bill who went out to the world time and again and he must have been wasting "his substance with riotous living" for he'd come home so many times without anything.

The irony of the analogy was that his sons intended to be nothing like him, but they too were wasting their lives and any substance they could earn on riotous living.

Her mind turned to Eddie. She cautioned him almost every day not to fall into the habits of his brothers. He not only reassured his mother, but he too took every opportunity to try to turn them around.

Nadine had taken all of her children to church throughout their lives. As they reached their late teens, each of the boys disappeared from the church house, preferring to be outside during the services with other boys. Eddie, however, remained at his mother's side during preaching even as he reached adulthood. Now, Eddie believed the Lord was leading him to preach and that thrilled his mother's heart. However, he felt the first conversions he must seek were within his own family.

Each of the boys often told both Nadine and Eddie how proud they were of their youngest brother. Their sincerity was evident in the treatment Eddie received when he tried to witness to them. Instead of belittling him, they listened patiently. But they did not change.

Nadine and Eddie settled into their new little home in Crossville. She missed the flowers and trees she had nurtured over the past years, but she and Roberta began planting new things and anticipating the beauty they would bring in the future. And each of the children frequently came for a visit with something beautiful for the new house – a pretty, painted plate or an electric lamp; Jimmy even brought a radio.

Electrical lines had been stretched down the Monterey Road before she moved, but she had not felt she could spend her sons' army allotment on wiring the rented house. The new house had power run to it from the very beginning and she thrilled to see light pour from the little bulb. Although she would never mention it to her children, Nadine was secretly longing for an electric range like the one Roberta had.

She chastised herself, *What a silly old woman you are. Don't you remember when you didn't even have a wood stove? Just count your blessings Nadine.*

Chapter 29

Bill Lewis grunted, climbing from the back of a muddy truck as the driver called back to him, "Old man, this is as far as I can take you. I think that Wallace man lives down yonder."

The stranger threw his hand up in an exaggerated wave as he pulled away from Bill.

What is this world comin' too? Them boys come home from France and think they don't owe their elders a bit of courtesy. Why do you reckon he couldn't take me down there to Roberta's house?

I should'a just stayed in Strawberry Plains. I don't think the winters are as hard in that valley. The thought caused him to smile despite his sour mood. He'd felt the draw of the mountain in the depths of his soul. If the truth could be told, he'd felt that draw every time he ever left this ole' rocky plateau. Now, he was feeling the passage of time and he longed to be home – and this was always home.

The smile lasted only a moment and he resumed his grumbling. Bill's monologue of complaints had started when some boy he didn't recognize in Peter's store had informed him his wife no longer lived in Clarkrange but had moved somewhere in Crossville. He could scarcely believe his ears. Nadine had always been home; she had always stayed right where he left her.

The slightest pang of guilt touched his conscience when he remembered the last time he left he had sold the farm away from her. He didn't bother to count how many years had passed since then.

Nadine would always wonder how he knew where to find her. She knew that he wouldn't even dare ask one of his children and most of the folks in Clarkrange would only be able to tell him she'd moved to Crossville. Nonetheless, when she stepped out of the kitchen, it was Bill she saw on her front porch; the long duster coat was the same he'd always traveled in, now showing much more wear. She couldn't help but wonder how many miles the tall shiny boots had made since last she'd seen him.

Her breath caught in her throat as she reached a shaking hand out to push open the screen door. He stepped in barely greeting her and sat down on the upholstered sofa as though he'd been home only that morning. Nadine remained speechless.

Bill showed no intention to try to catch up on the lost years, he only asked if the coffee was hot. Hardly knowing what to do, Nadine stepped into her cheery kitchen to get him a cup. Before she could return to him, she heard Eddie bound in the door. The ensuing silence quickened Nadine's steps from the kitchen and she found Eddie frozen just inside the door.

"Bill, this is your youngest son, Eddie. I don't expect you would recognize him."

Bill only nodded at the young man.

Nadine could read the questions in Eddie's eyes. Many times he had longed to know his father but his brothers and sisters repeatedly told him he was better off if he never knew the old man. Nadine secretly wondered if they were right, but of course she would never say so. Still, she could see that Eddie did not carry the bitterness her other sons did. And, while she couldn't blame the drinking on Bill for he'd never shown them that example, she did wonder if they would be so prone to it if they'd had a father who gave them the support they needed.

The question burning in Nadine's mind now was whether Eddie was alone. He didn't have a car of his own and she knew he'd been working with Jerry today on a construction job he had gotten. As calmly as possible, she asked Eddie, "Did you ride with Jerry?"

Eddie answered without taking his eyes off his father, "Yeah, he stopped to speak to Lenny."

Again the breath caught in Nadine's throat; her hand unconsciously clasped her neck as though she could force herself to breath.

Bill noticed her discomfort. "Ain't goin' t'be no trouble with that boy Nadine."

How could she make him understand that Jerry was not just a boy, he was a grown man seasoned by Army life and toughened by war. He'd worked in log woods that strengthened muscles and he chose to spend his time among ruffians and drunkards. What must she do? She was torn between a husband she vowed to love, honor and obey and her son who had supported and cared for her for years.

Before she could think of what must be done, Jerry was on the porch. He had to push Eddie aside to get into the door. As he opened his mouth to tease his brother, Bill caught his eye. Tension rose in the room like a flooding river. Eddie sensed it too and knew he must act.

In an instant Eddie put a strong yet gentle hand on Jerry's arm, gripping the tricep chiseled to stone by his carpentry and logging work. Eddie spoke his first words to his father, "We're surprised to see you, Sir. Were you planning to stay long?"

Bill was shocked by the forthright question; no one ever asked about his plans. "Awhile I guess," was his only answer.

Jerry pulled against his brother's grasp; Eddie continued calmly, "I guess it's really Jerry's and Lou's house since they built it. We'll need to talk with them."

Bill cursed and grumbled; he complained that he hadn't even gotten the coffee he'd asked for and he wondered why Nadine would let these upstarts decide what happened in her house. Then he began to play to Nadine's sense of responsibility.

"This rheumatism has been on me solid for a month now. My legs ache somethin' fierce. I guess I've just got too old to flop around like I once did. Need to settle in and let my woman take care of me. Now, you don't mind that do you Nadee?" Bill flashed a smile at Nadine that further bewildered her. She'd scarcely seen the man smile since the day she married him.

She could only muster a slight shake of her head to assure him she would not mind caring for her husband.

Eddie's tight hold had served to calm Jerry somewhat. One look at his mother told him she truly did feel a sense of responsibility to Bill. In an instant he made the decision to bear this unpleasant burden himself rather than subjecting his mother any further. Moreover, he reasoned he was protecting Eddie, the family's pride and joy. Jerry could not subject him to the overbearing rule that he'd grown up under; could not ask Eddie to have everything he worked for ripped from his grasp on his father's whim.

"Get up. You'll come with me. You are my father and I'll find a place for you."

Something in his tone told Bill not to argue with him. He remembered a similar tone in Lou's voice years ago, the last time he'd seen Lou.

Jerry took Bill with him and he would never again set foot in Nadine's home. Some agreement was reached without her knowledge and the next she heard of her estranged husband, he was living in a back room at the little general store Jerry had recently opened in Campground. Over the next years, he moved among his children's houses where he was given room and board, never finding a home and seeming content to accept their care without returning either money or love. For the rest of Nadine's life, she would see her husband only when she happened to be visiting with the particular child who was keeping him at the moment.

Nadine's home overflowed with her children and grandchildren. The little house fairly bulged with the joy that filled it. She often expressed to Roberta that she felt she was a burden to them since they continued to pay her daily expenses. But the family relied on their mother for everything from babysitting to mending, from homemade preserves to a strong shoulder and godly advice whenever they needed it.

THE END

A Note from the Author

The fictional character, Bill Lewis, spent his life searching for joy and peace. While he traveled, ate in fine restaurants, met all kinds of different people and enjoyed professional success his wife Nadine had just what he was looking for despite living in utter poverty. She had the peace of God.

We all long for that peace, whether we recognize it or not. It is simply something God has put in everyone – a need for God. If you have never accepted Jesus Christ as your personal savior, it is my prayer that you will do so today. It is as simple as ABC:

Accept that you are a sinner; repent and turn away from your sin. (Romans 3:23)

Believe that Jesus Christ is the Son of God and that He died to pay for your sins. (Romans 5:8)

Commit your life to God and ask Jesus to be your Lord and Savior. (Romans 10:9,10)

Neither I nor this book is affiliated with this site, but www.needhim.org is an excellent place to learn more about experiencing the peace of God through Jesus Christ our Lord.

Thank you so much for taking the time to read *Replacing Ann*. I have offered this novella as a means of introducing my work to you and I dearly hope you've enjoyed it.

Now I need your help. Please take a moment to write a review on Amazon.com so other folks know that you enjoyed the book. Also, please pass the word along that *Replacing Ann* is available on Amazon.

Please visit my blog at: www.TennesseeMountainStories.com for mountain legends, short stories and history about the beautiful Cumberland Plateau.

About the Author

A native of Tennessee's Cumberland Plateau, Beth Durham's novels draw both characters and plots from the region's rich oral history. She now lives near Chattanooga, Tennessee with her husband and children.

Beth writes Christian fiction and blogs weekly at www.TennesseeMountainStories.com about the legends and lessons from her beloved mountain home.